Also by Carl Dane:

Hawke and Carmody Western Novels
Valley of the Lesser Evil
Canyon of the Long Shadows
Rage under the Red Sky

Rapid Fire Reads (short books)
Delta of the Dying Souls
The Mountain of Slow Madness

Copyright © 2018 Carl Dane
All rights reserved.
Published by Raging Bull Publishing
www.ragingbullpublishing.com

Follow Carl Dane at:
www.carldane.com

First edition
No part of this book may be used or reproduced in any manner
whatsoever without the prior written permission of the publisher,
except in the case of brief quotations embodied in reviews.

This is a work of fiction. Names, characters, businesses, places,
events and incidents are either the products of the author's imagi-
nation or used in a fictitious manner. Any resemblance to actual
persons, living or dead, or actual events is purely coincidental.

ISBN: 978-1-9997600-7-6

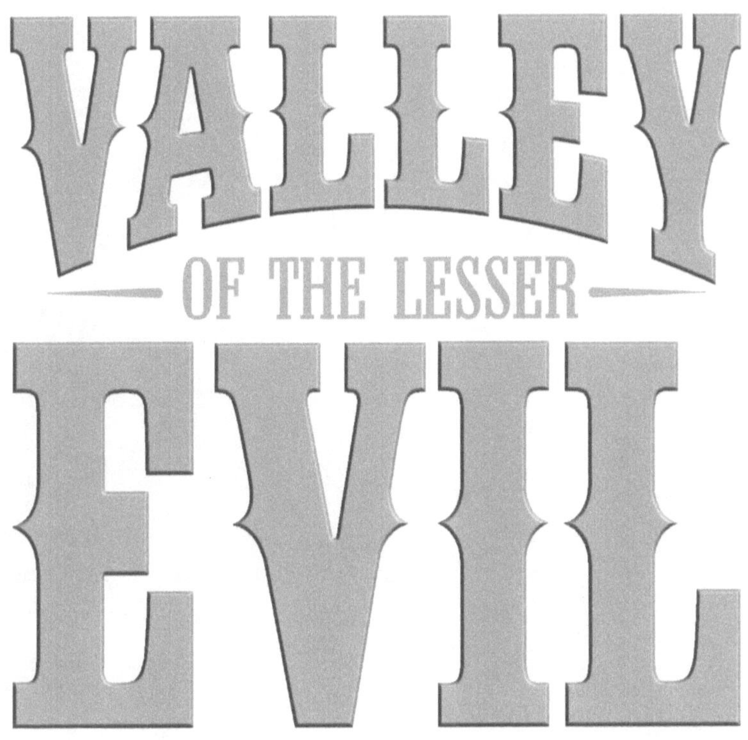

VALLEY OF THE LESSER EVIL

A HAWKE & CARMODY WESTERN NOVEL

CARL DANE

RAGING BULL PUBLISHING

Dedication

To Cathy, Carl and Mark.
With love.

Chapter 1

rs. Adler tried to keep a poker face when I point-blank offered to do her killing for her. She wasn't very good at it, and didn't blink for so long it must have actually *hurt*. I read something into the fact that she was trying to keep from *being* read: She was over her head and scared.

I'm pretty good at reading people, which is one reason I am, most improbably, still alive.

She hadn't come right out and asked me to kill anybody but these things always wind up with somebody dead and I like to start the game with all the cards on the table. After a full minute she gave up and blinked, and then said what I expected, what I usually hear, in some version or another.

"But...you seem like a nice man. I mean, for someone who kills for a living."

Now, part of that's true and part isn't, and I'll get to the distinction in a minute. First things first, though. My name is Josiah Hawke. I was a professor before the war. I taught philosophy, mostly, and some politics, at a small college in the south end of Illinois. It was the kind of place where kids from rich families orbited for a while before moving on to careers in law or the military or politics. I was never really poor but certainly not rich, coming from a long line of bankrupt blacksmiths and foreclosed farmers and the like.

I was largely self-taught. What I lack in breeding and book-learning I compensated for by being a quick study. I wasn't a bad teacher, and I liked the work.

But things changed for me and a few million other people in 1861, when I joined up with the 6th Illinois Cavalry, where I developed a set of unusual skills that has kept me gainfully and legally – for the most part, depending on semantics – employed ever since.

"I'm not necessarily hiring you to *kill* anybody," Mrs. Adler said, after I'd waited her out and she couldn't take the silence any longer. Most people hate awkward pauses and likely as not they'll blurt out what you want to know without you having to ask.

"Just…if it happens," she said. "If you have to. If it's self-defense. I mean, if there's no choice."

"There usually isn't."

Her cigar-store-Indian expression melted away and she looked scared and confused. In other words, like a normal person in her situation.

"Look, please, I don't know what to do. This was a peaceful town until the marshal was killed. It was just in the last couple of weeks everything turned strange, and that's when Billy told me to contact you if anything happened to him. He said you'd fix things. Those were his words exactly. You'd *fix* things."

I regarded her silently a while and let her figure out what to say next. She was a beautiful woman, to be sure, though she wasn't a kid by any stretch. I pegged her to be about my age, 40 or so. Her eyes were as blue and clear as a shallow lake. Her hair was a buttery yellow streaked with a little bit of glossy silver, not the kind of rusty steel gray that shows in my beard when I let it grow out. She had lines around her eyes and mouth, but they were like fine etchings in a coin, not the claw marks that life sometimes ravages into the faces of women in her line of work.

She couldn't take it any longer and blurted out what was on her mind. "I didn't mean to doubt you," she continued. "Billy told me you were the toughest man in his unit, and the smartest. I just meant that you don't look like a killer."

I nodded and told her that was one reason why I am so good at what I do.

"And you," I added, "don't look like a whore."

She thought about that for a second. I'd said it to test her. You learn a little more about people when you prod them.

"That," she said without irony or anger, "was why I was so popular."

And with that, the tension broke and we got down to business.

Mrs. Adler needed me to fix her problem with the goons and gunmen who had swooped in on her establishment, the Silver Spoon, a second-rate bar and bordello in what appeared to be the decidedly third-rate Texas Hill Country town of Shadow Valley. Her customers were being scared away, she said, and her help harassed. A giant goon they called Toad stood sentry and manhandled anyone brave or foolish enough to head toward her door.

The trouble, she said, seemed to be orchestrated from the only other bar in town, the Full Moon.

The owner was named Eddie Moon, hence the name of the joint. Moon wanted to buy her out, and had made several offers, she said. Good offers, but not enough to make her sell. She couldn't sell, she told me, partly because this was all she had and she didn't want to start over.

I didn't think I was getting the whole story, but I couldn't get anything more out of her and sensed that if I pressed more she would shut down entirely. It could be true: Preserving property and a way of life have motivated people to do far crazier things than holding on to a bar and whorehouse, and I've done some pretty foolish things on principle myself, including coming to this town and offering to hire on as marshal.

The pay was not much of an inducement – fifteen dollars a week plus fees for serving papers and collecting taxes – but the badge would give me some latitude and some legal cover when somebody wound up dead. I also wanted an agreement in writing that despite holding office, the town will still let me collect, personally, the five thousand dollar reward being offered by the state for the capture or killing of the murderer of Marshal Billy Gannon.

Bounties are a long shot but almost always worth a try, and in any event I owed it to Billy. He'd been my captain in the war and probably saved my life more times than I had saved his. Whoever managed to kill Billy would not be easy to catch, because Billy was one of the cagiest men I've ever known, and that was truly saying something.

The badge and the contract would probably be no problem, Mrs. Adler assured me, but the town council would take some convincing before hiring me because they were as scared as she was of the new thugs in town, and didn't want to incur their wrath by hiring a marshal if that marshal really couldn't protect them.

So we had a chicken-and-egg dilemma. A real problem, to be sure, if Mrs. Adler was the bravest member of the town council. She told me she inherited, in an informal way, her husband's seat after he disappeared several months ago.

The disappearing-husband scenario was a new rabbit hole, but I wasn't in the mood to dive down it because I was already losing patience.

I would have gladly walked away at that moment. This, certainly, was not a plum job. But I was on the hook to Billy Gannon, even in death.

"Tell anyone involved in the decision concerning whether I'm up to the job to be outside the Silver Spoon at seven," I told her as I slid my chair back. "They don't have to meet or talk or be seen. They can even look out a window as long as they can see your front entrance. I'll reassure them as to the soundness of their investment. Then you all decide what you want to do. I'll be back here tomorrow at nine and we can either sign the papers or say our farewells."

I dropped my horse off at the hostler and checked into the hotel and prepared to get down to business.

Now, about that business: What Mrs. Adler said about me was only partly correct. I *am* a nice guy when I'm dealing with nice people. I'm polite to old folks and gentle with children. I've never run a horse to death, and in fact I love animals, even though I also love them medium rare, which is what I believe Aristotle would have defined as a conflict of virtues. At least that's what I'd told my students in another lifetime.

I do my best to cope with moral dilemmas and stick to my moral code as best I can while practicing my profession.

As Billy told Mrs. Adler, I make my living by fixing things. I fix bad situations for good people, or at least people who I think have more good in them than bad. I enforce the law on occasion. Sometimes I kill people, but for the record, I don't kill for a living any more.

Nowadays, I do it for fun.

Chapter 2

After dinner I started scouting the Silver Spoon, and while I couldn't identify the whole cast of characters, nor immediately separate the bad guys from the good, I figured my first logical move would be to deal with this fellow named Toad.

I'm not sure if that was a name anybody called him to his face but it fit. He had oval-shaped eyes that bugged out, no neck to speak of, and a vague reptilian expression. He was also swelled-up like a toad. He was at least six-foot-five and three hundred pounds, most of it muscle. I noticed that he rolled his sleeves up past his shoulders to show off his meaty arms, even though it was a chilly late-October evening. When he thought nobody was looking he wrapped his arms around his chest for warmth.

I watched Toad for half an hour. He appeared to be the point man for the harassment operation Mrs. Adler told me was headquartered down the street at the Full Moon, a bar, casino, and whorehouse. I hadn't seen that place yet; I'd need to scout it soon.

Toad spent his time lumbering back and forth in front of the batwing doors of the Silver Spoon. He veered toward anyone who even looked like he might even be *thinking* about heading toward the entrance. While most of the passersby, cowhands and miners and such, must have been mighty thirsty or horny or both, every one of them subtly changed direction and kept on walking – like Toad exercised some sort of reverse gravity that altered their orbits.

Toad was wearing a gun. I was not. Not tonight, anyway. Gunplay was – for now – the last thing I wanted. Only in those dime novels does a lone gunman shoot it out with an entire town and emerge unventilated.

I would make my point with my fists, and while there's no guarantee that guns won't come into play during a hand-to-hand dust-up, it doesn't usually happen. Even the lowest species of thugs usually have too much pride to pull iron at a fistfight – at least when there is a crowd watching. In all my prizefights I only remember gunplay twice, and never involving me or the other fighter. It was a betting dispute both times, and I guess you could say that both times all parties lost, winding up either dead or in jail.

I'd had about a hundred bareknuckle prize bouts, fought under different rules or sometimes no real rules to speak of. I replayed a few of them in my mind while I leaned against a post and surveilled the Silver Spoon.

Prizefighting was an odd profession for a teacher and soldier, and it started by accident, on the same night my teaching career ended, a month to the day after my unit was discharged.

I had killed my opponent in my first fight. I didn't set out to kill him, but neither did I show much concern for his welfare after he'd tried to gouge my eye out. He'd been a strongman and fighter with one of those traveling shows, and he goaded me – in front of a local crowd of friends and students – into accepting a challenge of his hundred dollars versus my ten that I couldn't last two rounds.

Another man's goading never bothered me that much because I know it's generally a tool to try to manipulate me, and if I ignore it, I win. The money was good but not enough to risk a beating. I'd stepped into that circle because something was missing in my life after my discharge. I'm not saying I *liked* the war – no sane man would even think that. And I'm not saying that I was bored, exactly, after coming back to the classroom.

It's just that a part of me woke up from hibernation when that carnival pug called me out.

I assume he picked me because I was the biggest man in the crowd. It was a small crowd in terms of number and size because I'm not all that big. I'm a little over six feet and on the lean side, but I have broad shoulders and long arms and big hands. There are plenty of bigger and stronger men, but during the war I was in a very special unit where I picked up a world of experience fighting with guns, knives, fists, and – most importantly – my head.

The carnie pug was strong and fast, and moved with a grace that you wouldn't expect, given his bulk. I pretended to be afraid and danced with him until I figured out the steps to his dance that he repeated, without being able to discern his own pattern, like clockwork. It had the rhythm of the one-two-three of a waltz: Left jab toward my head, right to my body, and then a roundhouse right brought up to my head when I lowered my arm to protect my body. About the fifth time he'd stamped out the routine and began to throw his low right toward my ribs I hooked over the top and caught him on the point of the jaw.

When he wobbled back to his feet he was badly hurt and couldn't make his legs work right. I don't know why, but a blow on the point of the jaw will do that – make your legs fall asleep. He stalled, wrapping me in a bear hug, which is technically against the rules but given the circumstances, I could live with his transgression. But when he bit me and stuck his thumb in my eye I took strong exception, so I worked on his ribs until he could not hold his hands up any more and then I clubbed him to the head a dozen times with everything I had, even getting in three hard shots while he was in the process of toppling to the dust. He fell face-down and never got up.

Prizefights were illegal in that county. The law generally looked the other way but not, apparently, when someone wound up dead. I got out of town a step ahead of a county deputy and headed west – the path that led me to this strange spot in life, ten years later and ten paces away from this creature they called Toad.

Dusk was gathering, the streets were getting busy, and it was time to start the show. I needed to get people's attention and get this act over and done with quickly and dramatically. I certainly did not want a protracted roll-around in the dirt with someone who could, if he got on top of me, rip off my arms like wings from a roasted chicken.

So I walked right around him toward the batwings and let him make the first move, which I figured would be him grabbing me from behind and yanking me back. He was nice enough to comply.

I wanted to get him in the habit of pulling me.

I was taking a chance, of course, giving him my back like that. If he'd laid the barrel of the revolver he carried across the back of my head my brains would be a sidewalk omelet. But I knew he wouldn't.

I could read him.

After all, what would be the use of all that muscle that he took such pains to show off if he took me out with something an old lady could do if she could heft a two-and-a-half pound .45?

He spun me around and grabbed the front of my shirt in a huge fist. I pulled back, showing a little more strength than he expected, so he compensated by pulling me again, pulling me closer, hard and fast.

"Take a walk," he said, looking down on me. I could feel his breath and smell it, too, redolent of a strange mixture of cabbage and slaughterhouse aromas.

"Walk in the other direction," he said. "While you're still able to walk."

I said nothing, betrayed no emotion, and just fixed him with a level gaze. That confounded him, and I got the distinct impression he spent a lot of time puzzled about most things.

I kept my eyes locked on his, watching for his next move, but at the same time using my ears to monitor my surroundings. I could hear the soft shuffle of boots on the dusty street and a buzz of muted murmurs as a crowd gathered, as they always do, when there is the promise of some street theater.

So I backed away again, pulling hard, and fury blazed in his eyes. Toad took my shirt in both hands this time and pulled me again, back toward him, and then tried to throttle me by twisting the cloth.

"I'm going into the Silver Spoon," I said, in a very soft voice. "The place is officially open for business and anyone who wants a drink can have one. In fact, I'm buying. But no drink for you. You're leaving. Now."

The crowd hushed, some from surprise and some because they couldn't hear what I said. I could sense them leaning in, which was the way I wanted it. I had their attention.

Toad searched for a response but whatever machinery lay behind his reptilian eyes seemed to turn slowly and after a few seconds of indecision he settled for telling me to go fuck myself.

So I spit in his face and threw my right arm up, over, and across his hands, spun a half-circle to my left, pretty much turning my back on him, and pulled away with all my strength, going low so I could put the full strength of my legs into the effort.

I knew that Toad's reptile brain would telegraph his body to hang onto my shirtfront, even though his wrists were trapped for the moment under my right armpit and my spinning motion had imparted to me considerable leverage. I'd dragged him two steps in my direction and he almost fell forward.

If Toad were smart he would have let it happen because he would have been right on top of me and could have had his way. But the unfocused fury in his mind was instructing him to show me that he could pull harder than I could. He braced himself, let out an enraged grunt, and yanked me back toward him.

He was, in fact, monstrously strong – so strong that when he drew me toward him he probably tripled the force of my elbow as I uncoiled like a spring and landed it on his temple.

There was an impossibly loud crack and a crunch. More than a few onlookers gasped.

Then there was dead silence for a moment as his eyes lost their light and he crumpled straight down, collapsing into a pile of himself like a giant candle melting into a puddle of wax.

He was a tough son of a bitch, I'll give him that. Hurt as he was, arms and legs quivering, his head lolling on his chest, he kept repeating – this time in a strange mewling whimper – his instructions to perform that particular action on myself that as far as I can tell is anatomically impossible.

I kicked him until he stopped.

Chapter 3

Mrs. Adler kept her eyes fixed on me like I was a cobra poking its head out of a basket. She slid the badge across the desk with her fingertips.

"Here," she said, and snatched her hand back.

"I am overwhelmed by the majesty of this ceremony and flattered by your confidence," I told her, and it was obvious my sarcasm was not appreciated nor understood. She just nudged her chair back a little more.

"But before we seal the deal I need some answers," I said.

"You cracked that man's *skull*," she said, apropos of nothing. "My God. The *sound.*"

"He'll live. I checked with the doctor last night. He'll heal up no stupider than when I found him, which is probably not possible anyway. And I might remind you that it was he who laid hands on me. And I might further remind you, Mrs. Adler, that you hired me for rough work and knew what you were getting into. Don't you get on a high horse because I got *my* hands dirty."

"I know," she said. "I'm sorry. I guess I'm just tired of all the fighting and hoped against hope it could be solved another way. Don't *you* get tired of violence sometimes?"

"An inevitable part of the human condition, I believe. Plato said that only the dead have seen the end of war, Mrs. Adler."

She sighed and bit her lip, and we both regarded each other across the oak desk until her eyes dropped to her folded hands. The early-morning sun slanted through the window, a harsh and dissonant element in an environment that is more suited to amber lantern light. Saloons, even the back rooms, just don't look right first thing in the morning, nor do they smell right. The lingering aroma of last night's beer, piss, and puke is astonishingly rank at 9 in the morning.

"Please, call me Elmira," she said.

"Princess."

She began to stare at me again.

"Your first name is an Arabic word for princess," I said.

"You are the goddamned strangest hired gun *in the world,*" she said, balling her hands into fists and glancing toward the ceiling, as if imploring for divine guidance. "I just want to get these goons off my back and I get a head-breaker who lectures me about Plato and translates my name."

I held up a hand. "Fair enough. Let's stick to business. Look, it's my neck on the line and I have to know what's going on…what's *really* going on. You're telling me half the story. Now, I'm not saying you're dishonest. Everybody has their own recollection of events, but something you don't mention because you think it's unimportant or embarrassing to you could cause me to miss something and maybe get myself killed. So let's hear the story from the beginning."

She sat immobile as a sphinx. Sometimes, when you're trying to get someone to tell you things they don't want to tell you, you have to prime the pump to get the words flowing.

"But fair's fair," I said. "Do you have anything you want to ask me?"

She chewed on her knuckle for a second.

"Does my name *really* mean Princess?

Chapter 4

About an hour later I had extracted what I would guess was half the true story, which is about all you can hope for when you're pulling on a string connected to sex, politics, and murder.

And it was quite a story.

Mrs. Adler – Elmira – was captured by Apaches when she was a young child. The Apaches killed the rest of her family but kept her to be raised as one of their own. That was not uncommon. While it made little sense that some children in a family would be massacred and some raised as Indian children, I've learned, from books and life, that it also doesn't make sense to assume that everyone thinks and reasons the same way you do.

She escaped when she was eighteen, after her Apache husband was killed by Comanches. But her return to the white world was not a smooth journey. She was viewed as "tainted" – her words – and marriage and a traditional job were not in the cards. She played the only hand available to a woman in her circumstances.

Prostitutes, or as she referred to them, doves, had hard existences. I told her that her words reminded me of how Thomas Hobbes had described the despairing state of mankind – lives that were solitary, poor, nasty, brutish, and short.

She rolled her eyes and kept on with the story. She had a head for business and after a few years in the trade opened up a series of bordellos in which, if you believe her version of events, she took good care of the doves, seeing to their medical needs and protecting them from the more violent clientele.

Her husband – now missing – partnered with her to start the Silver Spoon, and turned it over to her during the war, when he served with a cavalry unit for less than a year before losing a leg on the battlefield and returning home.

The Spoon had prospered but not spectacularly so. It was a tough business. Running a bordello requires keeping a delicate balance of payoffs and power. Gannon did what most lawmen did to make ends meet: He took a cut for not enforcing the local ordinances against gambling, laws that many towns in the West have on the books but ignore when it is convenient or profitable or both.

Gannon was basically honest, she told me, and most importantly he kept the peace because he scared even the strongest and craziest of the local parasites.

But when Gannon was killed, all the predators slithered out in the open.

Eddie Moon, who'd always been sort of amiably ruthless, seemed to grow a mean streak and hired an increasingly devolving species of thugs to run her out of business. The campaign started with some local toughs, including the currently incapacitated Toad, and recently moved into a new phase involving some brothers named Duran she said were gunfighters up from Mexico.

Elmira stopped and asked me if I still wanted the job, knowing what I now knew. I thanked her for her honesty and told her yes. And then she told me there was one more thing.

There's always one more thing.

She'd heard rumors that Zach Purcell was somehow behind all this. When she said it, she unconsciously whispered his name.

Elmira asked me if I'd heard of Purcell, and I said yes, but didn't elaborate. We finalized the money arrangements, I signed some papers, pocketed my key, and left to check out my new office, pinning on my badge as I closed the door behind me.

Chapter 5

Except, of course, I had absolutely no idea where my office was. Going back and asking Elmira would have spoiled my dramatic exit, and I realized that I would not enhance my image by asking for directions.

I figured the easiest way would be to walk the alleys north of the town's main street, which was called Front Street, and reconnoiter from the back. About five blocks east I came to a brick building with the rear window covered with bricks of a lighter shade. That would certainly be the holding cell for the office. I would have bet that it used to be a window with bars, not an unusual thing in a marshal's office. But a barred window is an invitation for slipping in contraband – including guns – and I knew Billy well enough to know that he would have bricked that window over himself within an hour of taking office.

I circled around front, drawing the attention of a group of lean young men loitering on the boardwalk. I stared them down.

I found the marshal's office unceremoniously wedged between a cigar store and a millenary shop. There was a sturdy but crude bench to the left of the door and a fire barrel of water to the right. Iron lat-ticework covered the door and window, and a for-mal and ornately hand-lettered sign reassured me that I'd found the right place: "Town Marshal Of-fice, Shadow Valley, Texas."

The lock, of course, chose that precise mo-ment to be fussy, and I could feel eyes on the back of my neck as I fiddled with it for a full minute as I contemplated my face-saving move if I couldn't en-gage the tumblers. Should I kick the door in? Shoot the lock off? I settled for pushing the key far for-ward into the lock and pulling back on the knob and jiggling it, which eventually resulted in the infinitely satisfying sound of the bolt turning.

As is my habit, I opened the door by stepping to the side and pushing it open with an outstretched arm.

"You're a right smart fellow," said a voice from inside, a voice larded with a thick mountain twang. It came out: *"Yer a rot smart feller."*

I peered around the door and saw him sitting in the cell. He seemed not at all surprised to see me and picked up the conversation as if we'd just fin-ished lunch.

"Never know what you'll find behind a door – snake, man with a gun, man with a snake, or a snake with a gun." He raised his eyebrows and awaited my reply.

"Who *are* you?" I asked.

"A guest of the fine people of Shadow Val-ley," he said, "a town where, and please don't take offense, I would really rather *not* be. I would, in fact, rather be in hell with a broke back than here in this cell pissing in a bucket. But forgive my manners, my name is Tom Carmody."

He stood and removed his hat. Carmody was tall, maybe six-five, with a mountain-man build, lean with wide shoulders, thick wrists, and arms with ropy veins. His clothes were standard-issue trail-hand, and he had a scruffy beard that looked like it was made out of wire brush.

"How long have you been here?" I asked.

"'Bout a week. The marshal" – he eyed my badge – "the *previous* marshal, locked me up the night before he was shot. I had a little set-to at the Full Moon and made me a regiment of enemies all at once, so Marshal Gannon figured I'd be safer here. For the record, he seemed like a nice guy and all, and I am sorry for your town's loss, but I don't need no baby-sitting and I would just as soon be on my way."

I crossed over and sat at Billy's desk. My desk.

"You mean you've just been locked in here for a week? How do you…well…"

"To answer what's on your mind, there's a kid name of Wheeler who is some sort of custodian of the place. He lets me go to the outhouse in the morning and he holds me at gunpoint with his hands shaking. I ain't afraid of being shot on purpose but I would deeply regret cashing in my chips by acci- dent. Anyway, rest of the time I pee in this bucket and at night Wheeler goes to the restaurant, has them put stuff in a poke, and throws it through the bars like I'm some zoo animal likely to bite his hand off."

I laughed in spite of myself. "A *poke?* You mean a bag? I've only heard that word used in one place, Eastern Tennessee."

Carmody regarded me thoughtfully. "That's right. That's where I'm from, and clearly you're not. What brought you to my mountains?"

"I fought alongside some fine troops there."

"I take that as a compliment," Carmody said, smiling. "But now we must confront that awkward moment. I was a sergeant in the First Regiment Volunteer Infantry."

"The fact that we were both on the same side apparently accounts for the fact we won the war," I said. "Josiah Hawke, Lieutenant, Sixth Illinois Cavalry. But interestingly enough, when I rode through Tennessee I did so in a Confederate uniform."

Carmody laughed. He caught on fast, and I decided I liked him.

"You was one of them raiders played tricks all the time. Had the rebs going in ten directions at once. Had a piano teacher for a general, as I remember."

"General Grierson," I confirmed. "That's right. Unusual fellow. He was a piano teacher and hated horses. Probably the only cavalry officer in history more afraid of horses than of the enemy. But smart. He'd have us dress up like Confederate officers and order troops to charge in the wrong direction. Used to stick logs into the ground and paint them to look like cannons and scare the hell out of the enemy."

"Those are fond memories," Carmody said. "And now that we've had the occasion to relive them may I respectfully ask that you let me the fuck out of here?"

I asked him to give me a couple of minutes and looked through Billy's drawers. My drawers. As an Army officer Billy displayed something of a fetish for paperwork and I was sure I'd find a detailed arrest report. I did. It was filled in with Billy's small and precise printing, which looked almost like it was set by a machine.

"Well, shit," I said, putting the papers back in the drawer. "Your little 'set-to' injured *twelve men.* Broken jaws, broken arms, broken noses, broken chairs, broken *everything.* "

"They was cheating at Faro. Using horsehairs to pull their markers off the spot they'd bet on when the deal went bad."

"The report says the dealer asked you to leave and you went berserk."

Carmody held up a finger. "Now part of that's true, and part ain't. The true part is I went berserk. The part that ain't true is them asking. Nobody asked. They just laid hands on me. I would have left. I just woulda liked it to be my idea, that's all."

I paused as if to think, but I really wanted to fill the air with silence and make him uneasy and gauge his reaction.

He paused as if to think while he tried to make me uneasy so he could gauge my reaction.

"I would guess from the way you're dressed," I said, conceding that he could out-wait me, "you've been punching cows for a while."

"That would be correct."

"And you're not in love with it."

"A man does what he has to do," Carmody said. "There's worse ways to make a living, and I've done 'em all. I grew up living on the land sucking on frozen fish in the winter and eating squirrel jerky in the summer. Few weeks in the saddle don't scare me."

"Gunwork?" I asked. "Have you done that?"

"You mean hired out? No. You mean protecting myself? Some. You mean in the war? More than I cared to."

"Were you good at it?"

He nodded, and didn't elaborate.

"And what did you do in the Volunteers?" I asked.

"Scouting, mostly. Being where I'm from and who I am it's natural I'm good with tracking, good with seeing and hearing things, good with keeping my senses and keeping my scalp. Spent a lot of time on boats, too. Lot of waterways in my area."

"I spent some time assigned to a Navy ship," I said. "I hated it."

"Water's fine in whiskey. Other than that I ain't fond of it."

"The occasional bath is all right."

"I spent the last year all shot up," Carmody said. "Couldn't shoot, though I'm healed up good now. I finished off the war as a color sergeant."

I'd heard enough; he was telling the truth. The details weren't the kind you'd make up. He never said too much, so I knew he wasn't bluffing. He never said too little, so I figured he wasn't covering up. Not much, anyway.

"I always thought the color guards were the toughest men out there," I said. "I've seen them seconds from death and still pass the flag to somebody else before it touched the ground. Takes a strong man to put principle before his own life."

Carmody just nodded. "Like I said, you do what you got to do."

I stood up and plucked a ring of keys hanging from a nail. I guessed that the largest key would work the cell door, and I was right.

"I'm free to go?" Carmody asked, his eyes narrowing. "Something tells me it ain't that simple."

"Nope," I said. "Part of the deal I struck with the woman who says she's on the town council is the authority to hire a deputy. Ten dollars a week, plus ten percent of fines you collect and two dollars per arrest. No plea bargaining allowed. That's your sentence for busting up the Full Moon."

"You know," Carmody said, "you probably think I'm just a dumb country boy but I learned how to read and write – sort of on my own – and I've got a pretty good understanding of the Eighth Amendment to the United States Constitution. Mister, if *anything* qualifies as cruel and unusual punishment, this is it. But if I don't have to eat no squirrel jerky I'll take it."

I nodded. "Like you said. You do what you…"

He held up a hand, apparently saturated with my cleverness.

"Thanks, I get it."

It came out, *ahhhhh git it.*

Chapter 6

armody, Mrs. Adler, and I sat in the back room of the Silver Spoon and had a couple whiskeys. She was still wary of me but for some reason warmed up to Carmody a few minutes after I'd introduced them.

"Well," she said, pouring another round, "it's good to know there's two of you around in case there's trouble."

As if on cue, a bar girl stuck her head through the door.

"There's trouble."

I rested a hand on my Colt and jumped from the chair in which I'd been reclining; Carmody plucked up the lever-action rifle I'd given back to him at the jail and absently patted the revolver jammed into his waistband.

"It's the Durans," the girl said. "Six of them and they're all armed."

I shoved past her more roughly than she probably thought necessary, which I deduced from the fact that she called me an asshole and shoved me back. But I needed to get by her in a hurry and re-move her from the line of fire. There was no point in being sneaky. They knew I'd be coming and probably knew where I was. If they were going to shoot without warning they would have just walked into the back room and ambushed me. They wanted to lure me into a trap where they could claim I shot first, should it come to the point where anyone asked any questions.

Three of them were behind the bar and three were in a knot about ten feet away in front of a Faro table. They each wore two ammunition belts crossed over their chests. They all wore low-slung revolvers and one carried a rifle.

And the tallest one held a gleaming knife across the throat of the barmaid.

I stepped between the two groups, a seemingly irrational move that caught their attention and bought me some time while they contemplated the crazy gringo. It wasn't an act of bravado. They would be less likely to shoot with me in that position because any rounds that missed or passed through me would hit their compatriots.

They would see that and flank me in a few seconds, of course, which was the amount of time I had to figure out what the hell to do.

I didn't have to tell anyone in the place not involved in the fight to get the hell out. The handful of cowboys and bar girls all left their positions and poured out the front door like the place had been tipped on its side and they had slid out by gravity. In a few seconds it was just me, the six of them, the wide-eyed bargirl with the knife at her throat, and Carmody, who stood in the doorway.

"Let her go and leave," I said.

The tall one with the knife smiled, and not in a nice way. He bared big teeth as white as sugar.

"Señor," he said, "vete la mierda." He laughed long and loud, throwing his head back. He then spoke in thickly accented English.

"I joos tell you to go fuck yourself."

"I seem to get a lot of that advice around here," I said. "What exactly do you want? Money?"

"I want all of you to pack up and leave, that is what I want. Or I cut dees lady's tongue out from the bottom of her throat, wrap it around her neck, and then we do the same to joo."

Carmody cleared his throat.

"I believe they have a point, Marshal," Carmody said. "There's six of them. And I'm afraid there's only one of you because I didn't sign up for nothing like this. I'm sorry. I'm gonna take my sorry flank to starboard and let myself out the porthole. I do regret letting you down, I sincerely do and I hope you understand."

The barmaid, hearing that, looked over at him, bewilderment and terror in her eyes.

"Nobody here cares about your mountain-man bullshit," I said.

I mocked him with my best approximation of the peculiar lilt of East Tennessee, adding: *"and ah hope you unnerstand.* Get out of my sight. Now."

And then he slipped back through the door.

I waited. The only sound in the room was the ragged breathing and sobbing of the girl. It grew louder by the second until she began to wail in despair and terror.

The man holding the knife at her throat found her funny, apparently, and began to laugh again a second before I shot him in the forehead.

Blood, brain matter, and shiny white bone splinters covered the mirror behind the bar, which immediately cracked into shards and dropped straight down, like a gory cloudburst. His arms splayed out, he fell back, and the barmaid shrieked. The knife cut her – but on the shoulder, not the neck, and not too deeply, from what I could see.

The two behind the bar went for their guns but hesitated a split second, either because of shock or lack of a clear line of fire, or both.

The one to my left made up his mind and began a cat-quick lunge to my left. He'd be able to shoot from there and not hit the three behind me. Unless I killed him immediately, which of course I did. I led him a couple of inches to account for his movement and he obligingly ducked his head into a slug that tore into his temple and blew out the side of his skull. Then I shot the one to the right before he could clear his holster.

My shots had taken less than two seconds, I supposed, and I'd had the advantage of surprise, but I knew the three behind me weren't going to stay frozen forever. I could hear what was happening. The rifle had already ratcheted and I could hear metal sliding on the leather of a holster. I could sense the guns raising to be trained on my back and had that prickly electric feeling you get right before a lightning strike, or the second before you think you are going to die.

I ducked and began to spin, knowing I had no chance, unless...

Chapter 7

The two blasts from Carmody's shotgun were deafening, literally. He'd shot through the glass and shards filled the room like a swirling hailstorm, but in virtual silence to my ears. The gunman who had taken the worst of the buckshot looked down, looked up, and screamed. It was a tiny, muffled sound to me, like the cry of a bird. I didn't bother to shoot him again. He had pretty much been cut in half and could do no further harm and he toppled straight down, with what was left of the part of him that had taken the blast bending like a hinge.

The one to his right had caught the other scattergun barrel and was lying on his side, digging his heels into the floor and turning in a small, pointless circle.

To my left, one man remained standing. His left shoulder bloomed crimson from where he'd caught some overspray. His right hand held a gun, pointed toward the floor, but rising toward me in slow motion.

I'd seen that before, many times. The uncertainty. The gray, fuzzy world of indecision where a cornered man is torn between dropping the gun or quickly raising it and firing and probably dying in the process.

"Drop it," I said.

"Move and I kill you where you stand," Carmody said, leaning in through the shattered window.

The gun angled up perhaps a quarter of an inch, an absurd sloth-like creep toward death.

What was going through his mind, I wondered? A trick on his part, thinking I'd hesitate until he could spring into action with a quick shot? A derangement induced by carnage and cacophony? Fear of the humiliation of surrendering? Fear that I'd kill him anyway? Or was he bent on slow-motion suicide?

I played out the possibilities. Experience in killing hasn't made me immune to morality; just the opposite, and I don't think I am alone in that regard. So far, in my mind at least, everything I'd done had been justified. The tall one I'd blown away was holding a knife at a woman's throat. The rest had been reaching for their guns after vowing to kill me and I have no doubt that would have been consummated had not I fired off three shots without hesitation.

But the one in front of me was playing a slow-motion game. Should I shoot the gun out of his hand? An easy trick in dime novels. Not impossible – but damn close to it – in real life, even at close quarters. Wait for him to commit to raising the gun to shoot me? When the action was in progress, I might not be able to stop him from killing me, even with my three remaining rounds.

"I know what you're thinking," I said, even my own voice sounding muffled after the shock of the shotgun blast. "You can stall and think I won't do anything because you're moving so slow, and get that gun high enough where you can move quick and shoot me."

We were at the end of the game. He had only one move left if he wanted to continue the fight. And so did I. And we both knew it.

The barrel of his gun rose a sixteenth of an inch more.

Or maybe it was now an eighth.

So I killed him.

Chapter 8

One of the less appealing aspects of lawing, at least the type I seem to gravitate to, is figuring out what to do with the bodies. Usually, I'd store them somewhere until the undertaker made his appearance. Shadow Valley didn't have a full-time undertaker but, like a lot of towns, relied on one that made a circuit through the territory. The undertaker who had buried Billy Gannon would normally be back in a week but Mrs. Adler told me she'd heard that he died of a heart attack three days ago in the next county.

Billy had been his last customer, and now I was in charge of a pile of bodies in a town so god-forsaken that even the undertaker was dead.

Luckily, I was able to hand off two of the bodies to Felix Duran, who showed up to claim his brothers. One brother was the lunatic with the knife and the other the one with the slowly rising gun.

The gang was not made up exclusively of Durans, and from what I gathered Felix was actually the last of the brood. According to Felix, who spoke very little and glared at me with a flinty hatred, the rest of the dead men were ranch hands for Eddie

Moon, who kept some cattle on the land in back of his bar.

The fact that Moon was their employer in no way obligated him to dispose of the bodies and the longer I debated the problem of what to do with them the more they would stink, so Carmody and I dumped them in the cemetery without ceremony. We wrapped them in some blankets I found in the jail and buried them, as they say, with their boots on.

Carmody dug the graves expertly and in surprisingly short order. I surmised he'd had a lot of practice and commented on his peculiar ability but he didn't respond.

He did, however, compliment me on how quickly I'd caught onto his nautical code-talking. He'd assumed, rightly it appeared, that the Duran gang would never have seen a porthole nor probably have ever heard the word. Likewise for their understanding of port and starboard, a distinction which, despite all the time I've been forced to spend on boats and ships, I'm still not sure I remember correctly.

While I had it on my mind, I thanked him for saving my life.

Mrs. Adler, who seemed to have started to tolerate me, reverted to giving me a very wide berth. She'd not handled the carnage well, and after vomiting several times had openly expressed her doubts that it was, in her unusual phraseology, "necessarily necessary."

I reminded her, with some anger rising in my voice, that I'd warned her that such things would be inevitable, given the circumstances, but I can't say that I blame her for her reaction to the fact that I'd just turned her bar and brothel into a slaughterhouse.

Having said that, the Silver Spoon almost instantly became a very popular slaughterhouse. Perhaps out of morbid curiosity, or possibly because they felt safer now that some outlaws were flower food, dozens of customers elbowed in the next day, and the Faro and poker tables hummed with activity. I dealt some Faro myself early in the afternoon, and won a bit, which is not easy when you don't cheat. Faro is a game that is not particularly advantageous to the house, which, of course, is why so many dealers cheat.

I'd also spent some time trying to strike up conversations with the locals. But they were a tight-lipped group who seemed largely unconcerned with who shot Marshal Gannon. Some thought I was here to find out what happened to the mysterious Bannister Adler, something about which I was curious, but a topic that Mrs. Adler would avoid every time I broached it.

The druggist did spare me a few words but like most of the other people I talked with, he was circumspect in his conversation with me. I couldn't blame him or them, considering I was a stranger who had, in the space of one day, significantly reduced the population of the town. Bannister Adler, he told me, was a sharp businessman who, even after marrying Elmira, had been known to sample the merchandise at the bordello. And he liked them young. And there had been trouble in his family.

That's all he would say, and he summarily turned back to his task of putting pills from big bottles into little bottles, or whatever it is, exactly, that druggists do.

The barber speculated about the disappearance of Mr. Adler too, and wondered if Eddie Moon, who not only owned a competing bar but had land holdings in the area, was somehow involved. Moon, said the barber, ran a reasonably clean house and treated his girls well, but behind that quick smile he was as ruthless as any other pimp.

The barber said he knew nothing about the death of Billy Gannon other than what everybody in town knew: That he was shot in the side of the head while making his rounds the night before he was leaving for Austin.

I didn't know about the Austin trip, and asked why Billy was headed there, and the barber shrugged and clammed up.

I wanted to talk to Eddie Moon, but not yet. There was some subtle subtext here that I wasn't picking up and I needed to know more before I confronted the man who was trying to run Mrs. Adler out of town and presumably had dispatched the six outlaws who damn near punched my ticket.

I said as much to Mrs. Adler when I finally tracked her down an hour later. She'd been out riding in the property in back of the Spoon, and when she finally came back to the office her face was sweaty and streaked with dust.

Riding helped her think, she said.

It didn't help her talk, though, because as we faced each other across the desk she inched back in her chair and told me she had no idea what happened to her husband and changed the subject as deftly as a politician.

It was the damndest thing, talking to her. She was something beyond my experience, and that's truly saying something. On one hand, I didn't think she was lying. At the same time, I didn't think she was telling the truth. And while I couldn't put my finger on it, I had the sense that maybe she wasn't telling the truth to *herself.*

Short of torturing the information out of her, a prospect that was beginning to exert some appeal to me, I would get nowhere by talking to her. I picked my hat up off the desk and was ready to leave when the door opened and a girl of eighteen or so entered the room.

She had the same fine features as Mrs. Adler, but her skin was copper-colored and the hair coal black. The girl shared the same liquid eyes, but they were brown.

I stood and waited for an introduction.

The girl hadn't expected to see me. Her face registered surprise, and then twisted into a mask of maniacal loathing.

On Mrs. Adler's desk was a letter opener made to look like a janbia, an Arabic dagger with a narrow, curving tip. Either that it was a real janbia pressed into service as a letter opener.

The distinction became instantly irrelevant after the girl grabbed it and came at me hard and low.

I caught her wrist and pressed my fingers into the base of her thumb – not too hard, and not to cause pain, although I'm sure it did – but to dig into the nerve that would numb her fingers and loosen her grip.

She dropped the dagger and I let her go.

She grabbed her wrist, rubbed it, and backed out of the room, hating me.

Chapter 9

"She's a little high-strung," Mrs. Adler said.

"A little *high-strung*? She just tried to gut me like a trout."

"I'm sorry. She's troubled. You don't have children. You wouldn't understand."

"Up until a minute ago I didn't know *you* had children, until that maniac I assume is your daughter introduced herself at knife-point," I said.

"I suppose I owe you an explanation," she said.

"Do you really *think* so?" I asked.

Mrs. Adler, who comprehended sarcasm about as well as I understood this latest attempt on my life, looked at me soberly and concluded that she did.

Her name was Cassie, she told me. She was born when Mrs. Adler was sixteen. The father was an Apache who was killed by marauding Comanches a year after Cassie was born and about a year before Mrs. Adler ran away from the Apache camp.

Cassie was ten when Mrs. Adler married Bannister. Cassie and her stepfather had never gotten along, Mrs. Adler said, and after a while Cassie lost the ability to get along with anybody. Her mental health deteriorated to such an extent that she was eventually confined to a couple rooms above the Spoon. Most people in town didn't know she had a daughter, Mrs. Adler said. Cassie rarely ventured out, except, apparently, when there were visitors to be stabbed.

I turned the chair around and straddled it, resting my forearms across the top and leaning in on her.

"Mrs. Adler…"

"Call me Elmira," she said, I suppose in an attempt to lighten my mood. It didn't work.

"*Mrs. Adler*, we have a business relationship that involves me putting my life at risk. So far, at your behest and in your service, I've been attacked by a gorilla who tried to snap me in half, jumped by a half-dozen armed men, and now damn near gutted by – no offense – a *lunatic* you let sneak up on me without warning. From now on, I need to know everything."

"All right," she said, quickly enough that I knew she was lying. "What do you want to know?"

"I want to know what you know about Eddie Moon, and tomorrow I want you to come with me so I can talk to him and try to figure out what's going on in this loony bin I've gotten myself into."

I realized I was screaming. My hearing had returned to normal after the shotgun blast but loud noises still hurt and I didn't notice how loud I was until my own voice pained me. Truth be told – and I wouldn't tell her – I was as rattled as a draftee farm boy on his first day of combat. It's the unexpected things that throw you off balance. I knew there'd be trouble in the bar, and when it came it was sort of a natural progression of events, events that I've been trained to handle, maybe somehow born to handle.

But the doe-eyed girl who came at me with a dagger upset the natural order of things. I wanted to get my balance back. I needed a drink.

"Tomorrow we meet with Moon, right? No more surprises?"

"Of course," she said, more quickly than the last time she lied. "From now on I'll tell you everything."

Chapter 10

Eddie Moon betrayed not an ounce of surprise when we walked into the Full Moon the next day at noon. With Elmira in tow, I barged into the back office without asking permission.

Felix Duran, however, was startled and froze for a second before his eyes turned hard as coal.

"I expected you would come at some point," Moon said, as though I were there to sell him insurance.

He was a broad-shouldered blond man, medium tall. He wore a long black coat, a striped vest, a black cravat, and as far as I could determine, no gun. We sat at a round table.

Duran sat with us. I sized him up as he settled into the chair.

"I have to say you've caused me considerable inconvenience, Mr. Hawke."

I said nothing. It was his show now, and I figured he'd write the lines as he went along.

"It's not easy to find ranch hands," Moon said, "and you and Mr. Carmody managed to kill six of them."

He was smooth and could think fast, I granted him that. Admitting any connection with the Duran gang would have been the last thing he'd want to do, but I'd caught him by surprise with Duran in the room. If he'd claimed ignorance then how would he explain the glowering Felix at his elbow?

"I'm very much in the same circumstance as Mrs. Adler," Moon said. "This building sits at the southern tip of several hundred acres of ranch land, which I own and work a little, although it's not a full-time thing. Mrs. Adler's property is pretty much a mirror image to the south. At certain times of the year both of us need to hire some help."

I pointed at Duran, rudely, as was my intent. "And this is how your hands dress – with crossed ammunition belts and a .45 and, unless I'm mistaken, a foot-long sheathed knife stuck in his boot?"

Duran jerked as if he were ready to spring at me. I guess he wanted to see if I'd flinch. I didn't. Moon held up a hand.

"The range is a dangerous place," Moon said. "We're right on top of land that both Apaches and Comanches think they own and are willing to kill for – either us or each other. The rustlers are just as homicidal as the Indians. Look – how the hands dress or what they do on their own time is none of my business or responsibility. They're not my regular employees. I hire them for day-work, and they come and go."

"Your 'day-work' includes roughing up Mrs. Adler's customers and employees and damn near escalated into killing a peace officer," I said. "That peace officer happened to be me, so I'm taking this personally."

"I have nothing personal against you or Mrs. Adler. And I deny any insinuation that I'm trying to harm her business. I don't need to. It wouldn't make sense. There are plenty of customers to go around, and this isn't a particularly big place. Look outside. It's only a little past noon and I don't have an empty table. Why would I go to all that expense and trouble to close her business and gain customers I probably can't handle?"

He was right. I'm no expert, but like a lot of others in my profession I've filled in the gaps by dealing Faro and keeping the peace in these types of places. I know that a crowd that's too thick is hard to control, both in terms of cheating and fighting. You wind up with what I've read British economists are calling "diminishing returns," which is a pretty clear way of summing it up.

"However," Moon continued, spreading his hands and radiating that earnest, open aura so effectively employed by experienced negotiators, liars, and cheats, "it would make business sense for me to amortize my expenses running this place and taking over her existing operation, if the price were right. I've made several attractive and eminently fair offers that have been rejected out of hand."

Mrs. Alder took a breath and looked like she was going to say something but Moon spoke quickly. "I know what you're thinking, both of you. That I'm somehow behind the trouble at the Silver

Spoon. But why would I do that? Mrs. Adler, you can do the numbers yourself. I'd make a modest profit in the long run if I bought you out at the price I'd offered. But it would make no sense – no sense at all – for me to force the purchase by taking the risk and spending the type of money involved in hiring gunfighters."

He spread his hands palms up.

"Why would I do it?"

On that point I had to admit he made sense. Not that I believed he was telling the whole truth, of course, but on the face of it *nothing* about the current situation made sense. Kill a marshal, attempt to kill another one, hire gunworkers and thugs, risk a noose… to take over a comfortably profitable but essentially unspectacular business?

"Things around here," Moon said, "have just gotten out of hand for reasons I can't explain."

I thought that was an odd way of putting things, but saw no point in continuing the conversation. The information I needed would not come from Moon and certainly not from the sole surviving Duran, who make a shooting gesture with his thumb and forefinger as I left.

Chapter 11

A stranger stepped out in from behind the stable as I and Mrs. Adler walked back from Moon's office.

The man was decked out as a shootist, and his intent was clear.

"Step into the street," he said.

I told Mrs. Adler to get inside a shop and stay there, and I did what the man said.

"So it's going to be like this?" I asked. "You want to draw on a sworn lawman in front of witnesses? Even if you win, which you won't, you lose. You'll have a price on your head and you'll be hunted for the rest of your life, which won't be long."

That, of course, was bullshit, and I'm sure this fellow knew it, but it was worth a try. Carmody would certainly take up the chase if I were shot, but if the gunman had a horse nearby and knew anything about covering his backtrail he would be into the wind in seconds and in country like this – hilly with trees, valleys, and hidey-holes – even an experienced woodsman might never pick up the track. And the idea that surrounding lawmen would make it their mission to find justice for a marshal from an isolated dump like Shadow Valley was mere fantasy.

"Who's to say who did what?" the man said. "I just came to ask why you killed my brother."

"You're not a Duran. At least the Duran I know says he's the last one standing."

"My brother worked with the Durans. He was one of the men you buried without even finding out his name." He hovered his hand over the butt of his gun.

"What *was* his name?"

My question threw him off a little. He didn't answer but shifted his weight from side to side and flexed his knees.

"You're not anybody's brother," I said. "You're a hired shootist and somebody's offered you what seems like a lot of money to take another crack at me."

"I see you reaching for your gun," he shouted, louder than necessary considering we might have been reciting our lines to an empty house. When there was trouble, the residents of Shadow Valley could disappear as quickly as mice when you open the pantry door.

But I suppose he didn't see the harm in playing the game, either.

This was not the first time he'd done this, and I knew something would happen soon. As things stood, he'd established an alibi for confronting me and put on the record for whoever might presumably be listening that I was in the process of drawing first.

Then his hand snatched the gun with fluid precision, fast but not rushed. The draw is only half the battle. Gunplay is won by accuracy more than speed; there was no panicky spasm in his motion. In a split second, I not only knew that he meant to kill me but that he also knew how to do it.

I have an unusual motion that I sometimes use in confrontations where I'm separated by a hundred feet or so: I turn sideways, flip up the gun to my front and then flick my wrist to the side and shoot. It takes a toll on accuracy because a gun being raised straight up has a better chance of hitting some part of a vertical target – like a man – than does one that is being bought from the side.

But the advantage to turning to the side is defense. I'm two-and-a-half feet wide facing front but only a foot across when I'm standing sideways.

No matter. His shot went into the dust because I shot him through the heart before he could level his weapon.

A lot of dead men wound up that way thinking that a gunfight was over because they'd put a round in the other man's chest. But people can keep fighting and shooting on sheer reflex, or hatred, or both for a few moments after even a mortal wound, so I rolled to my right, came up on a knee, and shot him twice more.

His eyes were open but the life in them was vanishing. He fired a wild shot as he spun a quarter circle and fell to the ground.

I grabbed the Cooper Pocket double-action I keep in my left-hand pocket and spun myself around, a gun in each hand, surveying alleys, windows, and rooftops, and then I scuttled toward the cover of the nearest building. Where there's one shooter there is sometimes a backup, or friends intent on avenging what had just happened, and that's no time to try to re-load. The Cooper didn't have the stopping power of my Colt but it packed five extra rounds.

There were no second shooters, nor anyone else in sight. There was only a surprisingly thick cloud of smoke, the distant barking of a dog, and the whinny of a horse.

A second later Carmody called to me and announced he was coming around the corner and asked that I kindly not shoot him.

A door creaked and Mrs. Adler's face showed ghost-white in the opening. More doors squealed open and slowly a handful of people shuffled out onto the street to gape at the body.

Chapter 12

Carmody held the reins of the wagon as we brought another body to the cemetery of a town so woebegone it couldn't even replace its dead undertaker – this strange place where the town marshal spent most of his time burying people who were inexplicably lining up to kill him.

"You aiming to fill the cemetery up all by your lonesome?" Carmody asked.

"Not my idea," I said. "Seems like I don't have much choice in the matter. I just wish I knew what was going on."

"It don't add up, does it?" Carmody looked off in the distance as the wagon lurched out of a rut.

"No, it doesn't." I said, "Let's go through it step by step."

"Let's do that," Carmody said.

I lifted my hand and counted off the facts on my fingers.

"First: Six months ago, Mrs. Adler's husband disappears. Everybody's curious, but Mrs. Adler doesn't really seem to care. I suppose that's not suspicious in and of itself. Half the married women I know wouldn't kick too hard if a husband disappeared and left them a going business.

"Second, this Moon character steps into the void a couple months later, makes her an offer, which she refuses, and then turns up the heat apparently trying to kill the business and coerce her to sell, even though the potential profit would never justify the expense and risk.

"Third, Billy Gannon apparently kept the lid on most of this for a while, but somebody wants to drive Mrs. Adler out of business so bad that they ambushed and killed him. That's when Mrs. Adler called me in because Billy had told her to get me if anything happened to him.

"Fourth, since I got here whoever is behind all this keeps upping the ante, I guess assuming that once I'm out of the picture the pressure can really be turned up on Mrs. Adler."

Carmody pulled the wagon to a halt at the graveyard. "Before you have to use your thumb, why do you say, 'whoever's behind this?' You don't think it's Moon?"

"Not entirely," I said. "I just have a sense that he's along for the ride, somehow. He's no choir boy, that's for sure, but he doesn't strike me as the kind of person who would set up a series of murders, at least to take over a rival bar and whorehouse. He told us yesterday that things have 'gotten out of hand' and says it's for reasons 'he can't explain.' Does that mean reasons he doesn't understand? Or reasons that he can't talk about?"

Carmody turned in the seat and faced me. "I've seen people kill for a nickel, and I mean that *literal.* But for a guy like Moon, who has a good going business, would all this folderol be worth it? Hiring gunmen, risking a rope by killing a lawman, all to buy the Silver Spoon? Is it really worth that much?"

"No," I said. "It's not."

"And if he's willing to go to all this trouble and expense, and has the bankroll to back up all this insane mayhem, why not just offer her double, triple the price?"

"I thought about that," I said, "and I think it's because Moon, or whoever's behind him, doesn't want to attract attention. I know that sounds odd because shootings and fights and killing a marshal attract attention, all right, but when you come right down to it, that's the sort of stuff that actually happens in towns like this – a lot. You can explain it away. It's the same sad story repeating itself. But money leaves a trail. You offer ten times what a business is worth and pretty soon everybody's going to be nosing around trying to find out why. You can't explain away a crazy purchase. Also, upping the price too much would convince her *not* to sell. If I owned the Silver Spoon and somebody offered me three times the going rate I'd figure something was up and I sure wouldn't budge. I'd find out what the hell made the place so damn desirable."

Carmody raised one eyebrow. "So we're talking what, a lode of gold or silver in a secret mine in the land she owns back of the Spoon? I don't think so. I know this area, and the dirt barely has decent dirt in it."

"Maybe there's some sort of stashed or buried treasure," I said. "But I doubt it. I mean, things like that do happen, and I've seen it, but *somebody* would have heard a rumor, and there would be some gossip. It *always* works that way. I've asked about mines and treasure and such and heard nothing like that. Mrs. Adler says she knows of nothing valuable, and I while only believe half of what she says I think that half is true."

I began to dismount the wagon but Carmody held me by the arm.

"Look," he said, "we only know one thing for sure: Somebody wants you dead in the worst way, and that involves me because I can sort of tolerate your presence and wouldn't mind if you stuck around. And to be perfectly straight about it, if they kill you they are likely to do the same to me at the same time or in the near future."

I thought that was reasonable, and had no choice but to nod in agreement.

"So here's what I think," Carmody said. "This Moon guy and your boss lady are part of a bigger picture that we can't see. Neither one is acting much in the way of logical, am I right? Now, part of it makes sense. I could see a snaky guy like Moon trying to make things tough on his competition. That's business. Forcing her out and maybe buying her out makes sense, I guess, but now this cat-and-mouse game has turned crazy. That happens sometimes for no other reason. Two guys have words and the words turn into a fistfight and then the guns come out and other people get involved and before you know it you've got a deadly feud over something so stupid nobody can even remember how it started."

"And now we've got a whole cast of characters involved," I said. The Duran gang – and I'm sure there's plenty more of them – whoever this dead guy in the back of the wagon is, and maybe Zach Purcell."

Carmody held my eyes, and said slowly, thoughtfully, "I heard." It came out *ah heared.*

"A dangerous fellow, this Purcell," Carmody said. "When people round here say his name, they whisper. You know of him?"

I nodded. "We crossed paths during the war. Mean bastard, or so I heard from Billy Gannon. When Billy was wounded, right near the end of the war, they put him in charge of a prison, and Purcell worked for him. He'd torture the inmates. Beat a few to death. Billy busted him. Last I heard Purcell was a gun for hire, and a fast one. Got his own outfit, too. Big outlaw connections. Lots of fingers in lots of pies."

Carmody slid off the wagon and grabbed a shovel. "We'll put him in what I'm going to call the Hawke Wing of this pitiful little cemetery."

There was only one shovel and Carmody could dig like a gopher so I let him have at it.

"So, Marshal… if I may be so bold to ask, are you planning to stick around 'til the end of this dance? Even though you seem to have a big bright target on your back?"

"I am. For one thing, I owe it to Billy Gannon. The primary reason I came out here was to find who killed him. We've kind of lost track of that in the middle of this drama. There's also the matter of the reward money. Plus the fact that it's my job."

Carmody hopped out of the hole and jammed the shovel upright in the dirt pile. "Plus you *like* it."

I didn't say anything.

"Oh, I ain't judging you. Least not the way you think. If it weren't for people like you, and maybe like me for that matter, people who kill for the *right* reasons, the people who kill for the wrong reasons would have their way, and then some."

He began tugging the body, which I'd rolled up in the last blanket I could find in the jail. I grabbed the ankles. Carmody was looking far into the distance, at nothing in particular.

"I get the feeling you've done a lot of thinking about the right and wrong parts of this killing business," he said.

It wasn't a question, and I had nothing to add in reply, anyway. In silence, we lowered the body into the grave and Carmody covered it with dirt.

Chapter 13

We were getting ready to leave and Carmody could sense there was something on my mind.

"I want you to do something for me," I said. "Not now. On your own, when you have a chance. And feel free to say no."

"You want me to dig a couple spare graves before we go so you can fill 'em up later?"

I laughed in spite of myself. "Nothing so dramatic. But not fun, either. I have a strong stomach but Billy was a friend of mine. Digging the slugs out of his head might tell me something."

"Like what? One piece of lead's like another, and if it passed through his skull it'll be smashed flat anyway."

"Probably, I agreed, "but some slugs are bigger, some are smaller, some take on a different color when they're smelted. It might give me something to go on. Probably not, but maybe. Maybe not enough to justify asking you to poke around in a rotting body because I can't do my own dirty work."

"That don't bother me," he said. "There was times when I stayed alive by peeling back the rotten parts of any animal carcass I came across to get to something I could eat that hadn't turned to poison yet."

I pointed out Gannon's gravesite to him and we headed toward town.

Chapter 14

We both grew uneasy at the same instant.

Carmody jerked his head in practically a full circle and picked up his shotgun. I stood up on the floorboards, making myself a bigger target but gaining an extra couple feet of view on the horizon.

Neither of us had seen, heard, or smelled anything, but the danger was real. I'm not superstitious, but I believe that men used to danger develop some sort of awareness that's not related to the regular senses. And there was something going on here.

The Apaches appeared like they'd suddenly sprouted from the soil. There were at least five of them, broad, sturdy, and from the looks of it, homicidal. They were painted for battle. About five more were closing in on horseback. All were armed with rifles, lances and bows. They'd gotten the drop on us. They're trained to move low and quiet, an inch an hour, and in brushy, hilly country like this they can remain concealed until they're right on top of you.

There was no point in trying to outrun them in our sorry little one-horse wagon. There was also no point in firing first, as we were hopelessly outnumbered. But there was nothing to be gained by being taken alive, either, other than to learn what inventive tortures they could employ to entertain themselves for the rest of the afternoon.

"Don't shoot unless they make a move," I told Carmody. "If they do, I'll take the ones to the right; you shoot to the left."

Carmody said something I didn't understand. It took me a second to register the fact that he knew something of their language and was talking to them.

The big one, presumably the leader, laughed.

"What did you say?" I asked Carmody.

"I told him you said you would kill him unless they let us go."

"This is no time to fuck around. What did you really say?"

Carmody ignored me and spoke again to the Apache. The Indian's face grew stony.

"That's what I really said, and I just told him that you think he looks like a weak little girl and in a knife fight you would cut off his manhood."

"You are a real diplomat, Carmody," I said. I didn't look at Carmody. I kept my eyes on the big Apache.

"Is there something to be gained by making him more mad at me than he already is? Am I not getting something here?"

Carmody barked out more words, and the tall one barked back, and they barked at each other for a while until the Indian dismounted, his eyes afire, and waved the other warriors back.

Carmody lowered his rifle and looked at me, seemingly unconcerned about the circle of a dozen or so armed men.

"So here's the deal, Marshal. You just challenged the big one – his name is Taza – to a one-on-one. I appealed to his honor, saying after all we was way outnumbered and if he were any kind of man at all he'd accept your challenge. You win, we go free. You lose, we both die, which I very well imagine would happen anyway."

"Do you believe him?"

"They are always true to their word," Carmody said, jabbing the air with his finger. "And since they see we are outnumbered they realize it ain't sporting just to kill us, so the big one will be noble and will give us a chance by fighting you one-on-one."

I thought it was strange that Carmody chose this time to give a speech about Apache nobility but at that point I'd have to take whatever chance I could get.

Taza growled, impatient with all the talk. He drew a trade knife, not the crude pointed sticker they made themselves but a foot-long edged blade that gleamed in the sunlight. He pointed at my holstered gun. I knew what he meant and undid the gunbelt, letting it slide to the dirt. Carmody set down his rifle.

"There's a flaw in your plan," I told Carmody. "I don't have a knife."

He reached behind his neck and poked his hand down his shirt and retrieved one. I'd never seen anyone sheath a knife between his shoulder blades but everyone has their own ways. It was a good trick and if I lived I'd remember it. Carmody's weapon was what we called a side knife, straight and double-edged, popular among the Confederates and probably taken off the body of one.

"Nothing fancy," Carmody said, "but sharp and cuts backhand as good as fore."

The braves moved around us in a precise, wide circle. It occurred to me that they, and Taza, had done this before. Apparently, a lot.

There was no preliminary ceremony. He lunged at me, showing surprising speed for a big man. It wasn't a real attempt to cut me. He was testing. I retreated straight back in two quick steps, not a smart move but not a real move, either. Taza advanced, feinting low and then slashing at my head. I ducked and retreated, a strategy that couldn't go on forever because pretty soon I'd run out of room in the clearing or trip over something and topple back.

The circle of braves moved and reformed as we fought, as neat and coordinated as a formation of dancers. Taza was in no hurry and was in fact probably looking forward to the long, slow process of gradually disemboweling me and seemed to be genuinely enjoying himself as he danced forward with a practiced step and prepared to dart out with his knife-hand.

I didn't stand a chance at his game, especially as I was weighed down by my boots, giving up a couple inches in height, and having a blade roughly half the size of his. Also, he was an experienced knife-fighter. Many Apaches are.

But their fighting style is dictated by their traditions, and from my limited experience with Indians I knew that they knew little or nothing of striking. Punching him would be next to impossible because I'd have to come within knife range. So at his next forward step I moved to the side, which surprised him, and mule-kicked him to the short ribs.

The heel of my boot must have broken three of his ribs on his knife-hand side. I could hear them crack. Apaches are taught to fight without showing pain, but I could tell he was hurt and he withdrew his next thrust quickly when he found he couldn't reach forward without pain.

Around us there was some chatter.

I gathered I'd committed a breach of etiquette by kicking him but figured I'd better go with what worked.

Taza kept his knife in his right hand, despite the injury to that side. There was a fleck of blood at the corner of his mouth. I'd busted him up good inside.

He circled to my right, reaching forward with his left. His intent was to grab me and pull me toward him where he could do close-in work with the knife. He was betting he could fend off my slashes and wrestle me into a position where he could finish me off.

I whipped my right leg around and kicked him in his left thigh with my shin. It was a move I learned from a fighter who'd traveled in Siam. You uncoil your body and the kick lands, if you time it right, with tremendous force. Your shin is sharp and it whips deep into the big muscle of the thigh. My kick landed with a slapping sound and Taza was clearly stunned by the pain. But there's more to it than pain – the big slab of muscle gets paralyzed from the blow.

He took a step toward me but that leg didn't work anymore and he caved forward, flat on his face. He grunted and scuttled over on his back and reached for the hilt of the knife that he'd fallen on.

It had impaled him. He'd fallen forward and driven it into his belly.

Taza removed the knife, his face somehow registering surprise but not betraying the pain, and lay on his back, weakly waving the blade.

"He expects you to finish him!" Carmody yelled.

I hesitated. Under the right circumstances there's nothing in my moral code about going after a man when he's down because if you let him up he just might recover and kill you. I'd kicked the snot out of Toad partly for that reason and partly for effect, but Taza now presented no threat and I had nothing to gain by butchering him.

"They normally will not respect you if you don't finish the deal," Carmody said, "but that was a freak accident. I don't know what the rules are in this here situation."

"I don't want to kill him. Tell him I want to win fair. We will finish this another day. Tell him that."

Carmody grunted some words. I pointed to my knife and pantomimed falling on it. Then I snorted and shook my head.

"Tell him we will finish this later in a real fight," I said.

Carmody intoned a melodic string of three-syllable words and we began to back away.

The braves exchanged glances, unsure. Taza weakly waved his knife as more blood leaked out, soaking his tunic. The wound was closer to his side than his front, and while it was deep I didn't think it was fatal, at least not immediately. A deep wound can cause all sorts of infections and inside leaking and the like, but men have lived through worse and I imagined that his people have ways of dealing with knife wounds.

I picked up my gunbelt, walked to the wagon, and took up the reins as if everything had been decided. Carmody did the same, moving quickly but without haste.

We didn't look back until several minutes later. They had not followed us.

Chapter 15

Carmody was amazed that I could play the piano but seemed equally astonished that I knew nothing of Indian languages.

The upright in the Silver Spoon actually played pretty well, or I thought I was playing it pretty well, anyway. That was a conclusion perhaps hastened by the half-dozen whiskeys I'd downed to celebrate getting out of my last predicament with my scalp intact.

"Amazing you can tickle them ivories after busting your hands on so many heads," Carmody said. "I don't know how you can even make fingers work that fast, especially on them low parts with your left hand."

"That's an interesting point about music and fighting," I said. "As far as music, you can learn to do anything with your left hand as you do with your right hand, if you're right-handed, and vice-versa. Same with fighting. A lot of guys limit themselves because they think they are left-handed or right-handed and have to stay that way. Taza, for instance. He kept that knife in his right hand, even though he couldn't reach very far after I busted his ribs. If he'd trained to cut with his left as well as his right, I'd be a fillet by now."

"You are a clever one," Carmody said. "That's why I offered you to fight him and not me. I'm pretty good with a knife, but I figured you'd stand a better chance, being a professional and all. And besides that, I figured Taza would be more likely to accept a challenge from you because you don't look like much."

I let that pass.

"You know," he said, changing the subject without preamble, "I'm kinda rough around the edges, but I ain't no dummy."

"I know you're not. Never said you were."

"I've done a lot of reading and studying, sort of on my own. Picked up a smattering of languages to get by, and sometimes just for fun."

"I can get by in Latin and Greek," I said, regretting the words as soon as they came out.

"Well hot fucking damn!" Next time a bunch of Romans make us fight lions in the Coliseum we'll be in great shape. You are a handy guy to know. But in the meantime, if I was you I'd pick up a few words of the local dialects should you wish to survive out here."

"I think that is very good advice," I conceded, starting a new tune. "And I will follow it. I never ran into that many Indians. Only a few skirmishes on cattle drives, and I never really spent that much time in the saddle anyway. But I remember the songs the hands would sing. You know this one?"

"Green Grow the Lilacs," Carmody said without hesitation. "Irish. And before that you was playing a little Mozart, though you cow-poked it up a bit."

"I'm impressed," I said. And I was.

Carmody turned serious and looked straight ahead. He seemed to be mulling over whether to say something but decided not to.

Carmody was right about my shortcomings in frontiersmanship. What I don't know about Indians and trails and the woods is, well, *everything*. On the other hand, I know a lot about what I guess I'd call human moves – and even though I don't speak the language I could read Taza's reactions when I was talking to Carmody. You watch the eyes in a situation like that; Taza's were black and mostly inscrutable but he shifted his gaze between me and Carmody that I could tell he was following the substance of the conversation. And from his reactions I could tell he'd go for round two at a later date when he could carve me up slowly without being derailed by a freak accident.

Yes, Taza spoke English, or at least understood it. He was smart and pretended not to. Carmody didn't catch on, and as he'd saved my life twice in as many days I felt no need to make him feel bad about it. So I'd just let him lecture me on my linguistic shortcomings and move on.

When and if the day came when Taza spoke in English I'd pretend to be surprised.

Chapter 16

I ran out of repertoire a few minutes later and Carmody and I returned to a table. Mrs. Adler sat down with us. Carmody filled her in on the events of the morning.

"You should have killed him," she said. "When he said he'll finish the fight someday, he meant it."

"I believe you are right, and Mr. Carmody here was just reminding me – *at length* – of how little I know about Apaches. You both have a history with them – I don't know if you know each others' story."

They didn't know the other's story and they filled each other in. Mrs. Adler recounted her days as a child in captivity as she drank. Carmody, as he drank, told us about his years after the war when he roamed the plains buffalo hunting and lived on-and-off with an Apache woman.

I just drank.

About an hour later, Mrs. Adler had become positively loquacious, and after the second bottle of whiskey we shared we knew in great detail the story of her life up until about five years ago, and that's when her memory seemed to falter. I asked a few questions without wanting to seem too pushy, knowing that I would shut her down if I pressed too hard.

She gave me some half-answers and remained, still, a character outlined only in the broadest brush strokes. And when I tried to unearth the reason she wouldn't take a very good offer for the Silver Spoon and move on in her life she served up her rehearsed reply.

"This is the life I have," she told me. "And it's not bad. It's had bad parts, and the bad parts are still a part of it. But I'm the type of person who would hold onto a pair rather than throw one card away to draw to an inside straight."

I was going to tell her that what she said was pretty much what Shakespeare meant by writing that *conscience doth make cowards of us all,* but she didn't seem in the mood for one my of dissertations. And I wasn't sure, at that point, if I could get the words out straight because my lips had gone numb.

"Anyway, let's change the subject," she said, thickly. "Business is better, you two still have your scalps, and I just want to have some fun. It's been a long time since I had fun."

I raised my glass. "To fun, Mrs. Adler."

"Don't be so formal. Please call me Elmira."

"I am reluctant to blur a business relationship," I said, noting how hard it was becoming to pronounce two words beginning with *b* so close together in a sentence, especially now that the rest of my face was becoming as numb as my lips. I could hold my liquor as well as the next man but there comes a time when complicated sentences are too much of a challenge. I wondered if I could still perform all right on the piano, but decided not to test it. I wondered, too, if I'd drunk so much I was past the point of performing in any category.

***

The blankets and sheets were frilly things designed more for decoration than for warmth. The night had brought a sudden chill after the clouds cleared and the moonlight slanted in through the window and reflected off the cascades of gold and silver in her hair.

She drew up tight to me and tucked the covers around and under her as she burrowed her head into my chest.

"I guess this means we're on a first-name basis now," she said, and fell back asleep.

Chapter 17

T he gunshots rang out at dawn. I saw nothing from the window except fresh tracks from unshod horses. I could hear hoof-beats when I leaned out the window, and then I heard a woman scream.

"What the hell's going on?" Elmira asked as she shot up into a sitting position.

"Indian raid, I think," I said as I stepped into my pants and stomped my boots on.

When trouble comes when you're in bed there's always that awkward moment of indecision when you calculate how much time you want to sacrifice getting dressed. Lives could be at stake, even my own, but was the problem so exigent that it warranted me running out naked with just a gunbelt strapped on? It was too much to think about with a blinding headache, so I decided I should probably get dressed, and by reflex even managed to jam on my hat before I ran toward the door.

I just missed whoever had been downstairs in the bar. They'd ransacked the place looking for cash, apparently, but finding none settled for bottles of liquor, judging by the fact that two were dropped by the window, one of them smashed. The window itself had been torn out of its casing and lay on the boardwalk. I climbed through the opening.

The bullet buzzed by me and tore my hat off. I know it sounds like a made-up plot device in one of those dime novels but having a hat shot off does happen; I'd seen it many times in battle.

I had a choice of diving back through the window or seeking cover in the street. Going back through the window would take too long and leave me exposed, and in any event it would be bad for my image. So I ducked behind a fire-barrel full of water and hoped that the barrier was between me and where I reckoned the shooter to be.

A shot struck the barrel and blew out the staves in the back, soaking me. The bullet was deflected and missed me and probably wasn't traveling very fast after hitting the water, which absorbs a lot of energy, but my cover was literally draining away by the second and I had no choice but to rise up and take a shot.

They wore buckskins and leggings. They were Comanches on horseback, about a hundred feet away. They carried what looked like Sharps rifles, both pointed directly at me, a view that from my perspective made the Sharps look more like 24-pounder Howitzers. I fired all my rounds in their general direction as rapidly as I could and ran to the cover of an alley to hunker down and reload.

The Comanches hadn't expected my wild six-shot volley and they hesitated for a fraction of a second. I'd missed them all but hit a horse; it tumbled instantly, throwing its rider, and panicked the other two animals. In the few seconds it took for the mounts and riders to regain their equilibrium I'd reloaded and I sent off a careful shot around the corner. It caught the brave who'd been thrown to the ground square in the center of his forehead.

One thing you learn in combat is to not waste time admiring your work. I immediately shot again and winged one of the riders and ducked back behind the building, but not before I saw what looked to be half a dozen more buckskin-clad riders pour into the street behind them.

The hail of bullets actually chewed through the wood like a horde of giant, industrious termites. I could see sunlight slanting through the corner of the building.

It was time for a strategic retreat. Whether the locals would get out their guns and fight back was a question I couldn't answer because in the few days I'd been here I'd spent too much time playing detective and not enough organizing a vigilance group, or even the skeleton of a posse. So the fact that I was cornered was nobody's fault but my own. I knew that Carmody would come to my aid but I'd never set up any mechanism or signal to reach him. He'd taken a room at the hotel, which was past the knot of Comanches, so scuttling over there was temporarily out of the question.

The running gun battle had probably taken no more than two minutes. I'd have to find a place to make a stand and reconnoiter somehow with Carmody when he made his appearance.

When I heard the unique belching boom of his shotgun I knew he'd saved me the trouble. I couldn't place the source of the gunfire, and neither could the Comanches. They didn't panic, exactly – Comanches aren't known for wilting under fire – but they spun the mounts around looking to return fire but couldn't find the shooter. They bolted in different directions, so as not to make themselves a concentrated target, but not before two of them fell.

It was my turn to go on offense. Figuring I now had some covering fire, I ran back into the street and fired three rounds, aiming carefully this time. I hit one Comanche square in the chest, but missed the next shots.

It was then that I saw Carmody. He was armed with a shotgun and a rifle, and by now had slung the scattergun over his shoulder and was preparing for some precision work. The man is apparently part squirrel because he certainly loves to climb things; he was atop the livery, the highest point in town because it has a hayloft, and he could rain down riflefire at will and step back and be covered by the overhang when they returned fire. But from my location, he was *in back* of them, and we had them in a perfect crossfire: I could shoot without fear of hitting Carmody, and as he was shooting down none of his rounds could strike me unless there was some sort of a crazy ricochet.

And then the Comanches evaporated. On some signal I could not detect they slung their dead and wounded over their mounts, massed together, and thundered down a side-street. I ran to the corner and saw them already disappearing over the closest hill. I could see about a dozen of them. Some wore colorful headdresses, some not. Bodies of killed and wounded were slung on some of the horses. As I peered through the dust at the vanishing group of horsemen I noted that they all shared the same broad build except for one. It looked like a very young brave; almost a child. But at that distance I couldn't tell.

My horse was at the livery, and I assume Carmody's was, too. We could elect to follow the raiders but by the time we were saddled up they'd have a substantial lead and at that moment I couldn't imagine what we'd do if we actually caught them. Carmody could read my mind. He shook his head, I shook mine in reply, and holstered my sidearm. He slid down the peak of the roof on his backside and when he reached the eaves he handed me his rifle and I helped him down to the street.

I was going to suggest we check to see what, exactly, the raiders had done, but he cut me off, not, apparently, in the mood for chit-chat. It occurred to me his head was probably hurting as much as mine.

"It don't add up," he said, without preamble.

"What?"

"Why was they here?"

"I don't know," I admitted. "I was upstairs at the Silver Spoon with…well, anyway, I was upstairs and when I came down I heard a shot. I came down and the place was ransacked. Some liquor was apparently taken."

"Bullshit." It came out *bull-sheeit.* "Never heard of no Comanches burglarizing a bar. Stealing horses, maybe, but nobody touched the livery doors. They go after weapons, but I'll bet the jail and the provisions store are untouched. And sometimes they just feel like having a massacre for the fun of it, but that's a simple matter of kicking in doors and killing people, none of which happened or we would have heard something sooner."

"What, then?"

"You was set up, that's *'what.'* Somebody told them you were upstairs and they made some commotion to lure you out the front and they figured on taking some easy target practice. *Shee-it*, I know you're a professor and all but sometimes you are just too fucking dumb to fog a mirror."

I let it pass, as I did with a lot of his guff lately.

"So you think whoever got those Comanches to come looking for me is part of the same conspiracy. Whoever shot Billy Gannon, the thugs who tried to shut down the Silver Spoon, the Durans, our dead guy we just buried, the Apaches, and now the Comanches?"

Carmody shook his head. "I think the Apaches wanted to kill both of us just for fun. The rest of them, yes. Somebody's pulling all their strings, and whoever's doing that pulling is getting mighty frustrated. They keep upping the ante every hand."

"If we can find who tipped them off that would give us something to go on. Who knew that I'd be in Elmira's room?" I thought for a second. "Except Elmira."

"You have a deeply suspicious mind," Carmody said. "For Christ's sake, practically the *whole town* was in and out of the Spoon last night watching you stalk her like a cougar. Don't have to be no Pinkerton to figure out where you two was going to wind up."

"I didn't 'stalk' her, and in fact I recall that circumstances were just the opposite – "

"By midnight you couldn't recall your own name," Carmody said.

"I'm going to question her anyway."

"Here's your chance," Carmody said. Elmira was running toward us. Something was way off-kilter. There was stark terror in her eyes. Strange, I thought. The danger was over, unless I missed something.

"Marshal," she said, our first-name basis apparently a thing of the past.

"Cassie. My daughter. She's *gone. They took her.*"

Chapter 18

To tell you the truth, my initial reaction was to worry for the safety of the Comanches, but Elmira's anguish was compelling and it had now fallen on me to do something. Cassie was missing from her room, which Elmira told me was two doors down the hall from hers, and the room showed signs of a struggle.

"We'll go after her," I said.

I was going to reassure Elmira as to how it wouldn't be a fair fight, Carmody and me against only a dozen or so of them, but I was too hung over to be cocky and I faced a real dilemma in terms of what to do next. I could use ten men. Twenty would be better. But the local druggists and merchants probably would not be of much use. You never know, as the mildest-looking men sometimes had superior war records, but there was no time to figure that out. I suppose I could try to recruit a posse from the drifters who were in and out the saloons, but even if I could find them and wake them up, I had no way of telling who were the good guys and who were part of the growing contingent who wanted me dead.

The reality was that the Comanches had a young girl, who, despite the fact that she was a homicidal maniac, did not deserve the fate that could be in store for her. I say "could be" because it's a crap-shoot. I've heard of young people taken by Indians who were treated humanely and actually absorbed into the culture. But some were raped and tortured and killed.

I held out hope that Cassie was taken for a specific reason, as a bargaining chip, and therefore would not be killed. But it was up to Carmody and me. Assuming we could catch the Comanches – not a given because they tended to be expert horsemen – there still remained the problem of what we would do when we caught them.

Our only option was to track them from a distance and sneak up when they made camp. And then think of something pretty damn clever.

Carmody had no trouble picking up their tracks and we kept a steady pace for about an hour. They were not moving quickly, Carmody said, judging from the length of the horses' strides. We could probably overtake them, but the country here was fairly open, meaning that it would be impossible to sneak up in broad daylight.

Carmody's eyes remained glued on the tracks and he was unshakeable at following them. I could mostly follow the tracks, too, but not always. There were a couple spots where the prints and disturbed vegetation led to the edge of a stream but we were able to spot trampled brush on the other side.

Inexplicably, Carmody grew unhappier by the hour and his scowl deepened. Just when I was about to ask him why he was such a moody cuss he motioned for me to follow and angled his horse up a steep hill.

"Where are you going?" I asked, keeping my voice low, even though I didn't think anyone was close enough to hear.

"I want to check our backtrail. See if there's somebody following us. This is too easy. They *want* us to follow them."

I was surprised. "It doesn't look easy to me. A few times you had to look twice to find where they'd cut through streams or gravel."

"No. It's still too easy. These are Comanches. They can ride elephants through a mud flat and hide the prints. But they also know that anybody who knows a little bit about tracking, and a little bit about Comanches, would know that. So they're playing a game with us. They leave just enough of a trail that somebody could follow and think they're a clever tracker. Not so much as to make it obvious that they are trying to bait us."

Then the obvious occurred to me and my mood turned as sour as Carmody's.

"And seeing as how we haven't done nothing to hide our backtrail," Carmody said, confirming the obvious, "if there's somebody following us – which I'll wager there *is* – we're easy pickings."

We edged up a hill that got stonier and steeper the higher we climbed. Carmody pulled up under a broad live oak that would provide us some cover and pulled a brass looking-glass out of his saddlebag. He shielded the lens with his hand to prevent a reflection from giving our position away.

He handed me the glass. "Seven of them, I think. Dressed like those Durans who tried to take us out in the Spoon. Can you see them? Focus on that bald spot on the hill, drop the glass about ten degrees, and you'll see them."

Carmody's eyes were exceptional. My vision's good, but I couldn't make out the details of their dress and had to take his word for it. But he was right about the basics. A line of riders was moving single file about what I would guess was an hour's ride behind us. It could be seven. Maybe eight.

"There's about two hours of daylight left," Carmody said. "The way they're moving in front of us, I don't think they're in no hurry. They're interested in luring us in so they'll make camp where we can see them and hope to spring a trap. They figure they win either way. Either we'll catch up to the ones in front of us and commit suicide by Indian, or, if we don't, they'll just come up on our backside tonight or in the morning and pick us off. Frankly, I don't think our odds are too good either way."

"No, we can't beat them head-on. We have to come up with another option."

"Yep," Carmody said. "I'm sure we can come up with something. I assume you have an idea."

"I was hoping you had one," I said.

"I do: Let the officer in the group figure it out."

Chapter 19

I drew the scenario, what I knew for sure and what I surmised, in the dirt with a stick.

"We know the Comanches are somewhere north of where we are now," I said, scratching out an X. "They're waiting for us to catch up to them so they can capture or kill us. And they're using Cassie as bait."

Carmody nodded and gave me the look that I've learned means he thinks I should speed things up.

"And following on our tail is the Duran gang. They're a couple miles south. They're tracking us in case we get lost or give up and turn around."

"Correct. We knew that before we drew this little work of art. May I be so bold as to ask if this is leading somewhere?"

I told him I wasn't sure yet, which was the truth, and which seemed to satisfy him for the moment.

"But give me your best guess about a few things," I said. "You're the woodsman. I can find my way around better than some and as good as most, but I'm no expert and I know enough to know what I *don't* know. So first: The Indians are expecting us to try to get the girl. Will they double back and look for us? Will they keep going after dark? Or will they camp?

Carmody tapped a finger at the end of the line in the dirt. "They'll camp. They are surely headed toward one of their villages but I doubt if it's this close. Maybe another day's ride, or maybe two. They won't come back at night looking for us. Indians, as a rule, don't like to attack at night, although some Comanches don't mind. But it ain't convenient. Even the best Comanche tracker would have a tough time finding us in the dark, and they would be walking into our stronghold. Nope…they know we have to come to them, so they'll force our hand and they're holding all the cards. They'll camp, put up some sentries, and see if we try for them tonight. We *could*, I think. There's an hour of daylight and then twilight enough so if they move at the pace they've kept up all day we could catch up and find them. But then we're like a dog chasing a bear. What do we do when we catch it?"

"OK, question two: Will the Durans move at night?"

Carmody didn't hesitate. "No. They probably won't be able to follow the trail much after dark. I'm not sure they is good trackers to begin with. Gangs of guns for hire generally don't operate deep in this sort of country. And what would be the point for them? Whoever sent them told them they were a backstop, so my guess is they will just cover the flank and catch us if we slow down or turn around."

"Last question," I said. "Do you think the Comanches know that the Duran gang is in back of us?"

Carmody shook his head without hesitation. "No. Whoever's behind the whole scheme has nothing to gain by telling the Comanches there's a backup plan. The way I figure it, somebody with lots of savvy and lots of money and lots of good reasons – reasons that I just don't understand at the present moment – wants us dead and is taking no chances. They hire the Comanches to kidnap the girl and goad us into following so the Comanches can ambush us or kill us if we catch up. But if we fell behind or came to our senses and hightail back, the Durans pulling up the rear would finish the job. Smart. And just as icing on the cake, our deaths would be pretty much untraceable. Just another two dumb sorry-ass bastards killed by Indians or bushwhackers."

"Smart," I agreed. "And it would probably have worked if you hadn't noticed that the trail of breadcrumbs was a little too easy to follow."

"It *still* might work," Carmody said. "In case you haven't noticed, we are now between that proverbial rock and the hard place."

That was true. To be sure, they had more men and more arms. But *we knew something they didn't*, and in my line of work, that's the trump card. And I could think of a way to play it.

In the gathering darkness, I knelt down and drew out the plan in the sand.

Carmody said it was crazy.

And then he added that it was *so* crazy there was an outside chance we could make it work.

Chapter 20

In some ways, the least stressful part of battle is the fighting. The aspect that wears a man down in war is the waiting and worrying.

When Billy Gannon was captain of my unit he said that a lot – just to reassure us that we weren't crazy. Many's the night we spent camped, waiting to attack at dawn, or killing time during the day waiting to attack at night. Those were the times that ate holes in your stomach.

We had worked well together. Gannon had a real military background; he was an Academy man and knew all about tactics and training. He knew when to advance and when to retreat, when to hit head-on and when to flank. Maybe most important, he understood how to deploy men and convince them to go counter to every survival instinct bred into the species and run toward danger instead of away from it.

I knew very little of that sort of thing in the beginning, but in my own estimation I knew human moves better than Captain Gannon, so we made a good pair, especially for the kind of work we did. We spend most of our time behind enemy lines, and our job was to harass and confuse, and we were good at it.

I thought about Gannon and our group of raiders while Carmody and I killed time until dusk. It was a night like this in '64 when we were advance scouts trying to disrupt an army of maybe two thousand rebs ahead of a union attack. Our group of thirty or so advance scouts killed time until sunset and then spent the night lighting about fifty campfires for almost a mile along the face of a tall, broad hill to the north of where the main Confederate force was located. At dawn, we began marching through a small clearing to the north that we reckoned would be visible from the enemy's position. We marched, and marched, and marched some more. Thing was, we'd march, sneak around the back of the clearing, and keep the circle going for hours.

The confederates watching us through their field telescopes anticipated a huge showdown. They massed, ready to defend against what they thought were at least two thousand men in front of them, to the north. That's what the ones who were captured told us.

The rebel detachment was captured from the south, where the Union troops were really massed. They took them by surprise, and the battle was pretty much over before it started.

Things don't always work out so neatly, of course. But sometimes they do. We'd know for sure in a few hours, if we lived that long. Carmody and I rested, ate, watered the horses, and at about midnight headed toward where we expected to find the Duran camp.

Chapter 21

It was a moonlit night, and following our own trail back where we'd come wasn't so hard for Carmody. I couldn't have done it, but he could not only read tracks but seemed to have total recall of every twist and turn we'd made earlier.

"You spend enough time in the wild," Carmody whispered to me, "you get in the habit of noticing things. Your life can depend on backtracking to where you saw a water hole, or some food to forage. That's how my mind works."

I nodded.

"Now *your* mind," Carmody continued, "has been trained to work in a different way. I'll wager you remember very little of these here twists and turns and undergrowth that gets trampled and muddy parts that leave tracks and such."

"Very little," I agreed.

"But do you remember spots where we could find a good nest to shoot from, or spots where we could hide up high and have a clear shot at anyone who followed?"

"Five, with one coming up over the next rise. But I'm not sure if that gives us any clear advantage considering what we're trying to do."

"You never know," Carmody said. "Lots of things I don't know. Lots of things *you* don't know. But lots of stuff we *do* know that could be useful. Together, though, we add up to a very crazy and dangerous team, I'll say that."

I was going to reply but Carmody held up a hand and then stabbed his index finger twice into the gloom ahead. He's seen something that I could not yet make out.

Carmody pulled his mount alongside mine and leaned close, cupping his hands to my ear as he whispered. "Man standing, leaning on a rifle, maybe a quarter mile ahead up on that small plateau. A sentry."

I nodded and dismounted and told Carmody to wait while I did my business.

We had just crossed back into my territory.

Chapter 22

I'd packed a pair of moccasins in my saddlebags and changed into them. They made less noise on hard surfaces and gave your feet the feel of the terrain so that if you walked carefully with a measured step you could avoid putting pressure on something that would snap or crunch.

It took me about half an hour to circle around in back of the sentry.

I could have accomplished it faster but there was some important reconnoitering I had to do first. I found what I needed: a trail that was steep but not so steep that the horses couldn't handle it, with a sheltered area at the top and what looked like a viable escape route on the other side.

The "sentry" did not appear to be a member of the military elite. The man, of medium size and wearing a sombrero and crossed cartridge belts, stood leaning on his rifle for a few minutes at a time, looking mostly at the ground. Then he'd squat on a rock and appeared to doze.

I was good at what we called "sentry removal" during the war. In fact, I had taught the technique to my unit and several other commands after I'd put my own twist on the method. Sneaking up was the easy part, especially on a night like to-night, with a brisk breeze that produced covering sound, and a sleepy target who didn't really expect trouble. It was the final rush and finish that was tricky.

You have to cover the last ten feet or so quick as a cat and slip your arm around the sentry's throat and simultaneously jam the top of your head into the back of his neck. If you're fast and forceful enough your forearm chokes off his air and prevents him from making any sound. And if you dig in with all your might your target will be unconscious in a few seconds.

When I was finished, I lowered him gently to the ground, stripped his clothes, hat, and ammunition belt from him in less than a minute, and then double-timed back to where Carmody waited with the horses.

"Keep looking in back of you," Carmody urged as we rode. "Your life depends on knowing this trail when we come back, and it's clouding up so you won't be able to see as much later. Also, we need to high-tail if that guy wakes up and alerts the rest of the camp."

I was a little surprised at what Carmody said.

"That gang is following us so they can *kill* us," I said.

Carmody didn't get it, and turned to look at me. "Well I know *that*. What are you getting at?"

"The sentry. He's not going to wake up."

I could see in the moonlight that Carmody's expression had clouded. He didn't reply.

I broke the silence after a few minutes. "How far ahead do you think the Comanches are camped?"

"Well, they ain't playing hard to get, that's for sure, and they'll want to be in range where they can scout their backtrail and sniff us out if they get tired of waiting for us to ride into their trap. So maybe a mile. Maybe two."

"So we're guessing maybe four miles between the Durans and the Comanches," I said. "An hour or so with the horses at a slow walk."

"Half that if we come back as fast as the horses can go over this terrain," Carmody said. "It ain't rough, and I don't expect the path up ahead of us will be much different from what we've covered, but it's always a gamble at night. If we lose a horse we lose our scalps, so keep your eyes open."

Chapter 23

We smelled wood smoke and knew we were close to the Comanche camp.

There would be no sleepy sentries here. They expected we were coming, though probably not at night, and were not the kind to let their guard down. They expected an attack.

But probably not the kind of attack that was coming.

Carmody told me there would be a ring of silent observers lurking in the brush, waiting for us to attempt to sneak in and scout out the camp. Trying that, Carmody noted, would be futile.

"You can't out-Injun an Injun," is how he put it.

And I had no intention of trying to be stealthy. I jammed the sombrero tight on my head, rubbed the dark clay soil into my face one last time, and rode toward the fire at full gallop, firing as fast as I could at nothing in particular. Behind me, Carmody's shotgun boomed.

There were about seven teepees in the clearing. From my limited understanding of Comanches I knew that they were lifelong nomads and could erect a sizeable camp in minutes. I also knew that they were always on alert, and seconds after the gunshots buffalo-skin flaps of the teepees were folded back and hard eyes glared at me, completely devoid of fear or surprise. I surmised that they were keeping me in sight while reaching for a weapon with a free hand.

I wanted them to get a good look and held my position as long as I dared.

A slug buzzed by me and I heard the report of a rifle to my right. Then came the blast of a shotgun and a muffled cry from what I presumed was one of the Comanche sentries.

I turned and spurred my mount and rode as if I were outrunning death, which is exactly what I was doing. The horse gave an impressive kick. Both Carmody and I favored what were called Steeldusts in that part of Texas – quarter horses that were favorites on cattle drives. They were sure-footed. Over a short distance – especially the quarter-mile, which is where they got their name – they were as fast as any thoroughbred.

Carmody had lit out first and was already way ahead of me, which was the plan. He had business to attend to on the other end before I arrived.

I didn't hear hoofbeats behind me for more than a minute. We caught them by surprise because what happened didn't fit what I imagined they had been told to expect – a canny woodsman and an experienced military officer who would attempt a stealth rescue. The brazen and apparently insane gunman with a sombrero with blazing guns was not in the script and threw them off.

I kept the horse a little short of a full gallop in parts of the journey; one vine or chuck-hole could spell a quick death for me as I pitched forward on my head or an excruciatingly slow demise if I survived and was taken captive.

At about the halfway point I was on a rise and could see them closing on me, not much more than a half-mile back. Maybe eight of them single-file, moving with steady precision. I may have had the faster horse, but nighttime riding and tracking was their game, not mine.

My horse began to blow a little and I backed off slightly. Killing the Steeldust would accomplish nothing. And neither, ironically, would losing my pursuers.

I had taken Carmody's admonition to heart and memorized the landmarks: a stream, a lightning-toppled tree, and then a thick grove of willows.

And then I saw the trail I had scouted out before killing the sentry.

The Steeldust didn't like the steep ascent but I spurred him, and felt guilty about it, but he grudgingly picked his way up to a level patch of gravel that was sheltered by several large boulders. I dismounted and rested my elbows on the flattest rock and shouldered my rifle.

Down below, to the right, near where I surmised the Duran camp was, I heard what sounded like a Comanche war cry and a series of shots. It was, in fact, a real Comanche war cry although it did not come from a real Comanche.

Carmody found the steep trail based on nothing more than my description and was beside me on the gravel plateau before the first of the Durans rode out beneath us. They were riding full-tilt, guns drawn.

"Incredible war cry for a Scots-Irish guy from Tennessee," I told Carmody. "Scared the crap out of me."

"Good pair of lungs is an essential tool of the frontier fighting man," Carmody said as he reloaded his shotgun, his sidearm, and the rifle I'd taken off the sentry. I handed him one of the ammunition belts I'd worn crossed across my chest, the way the Duran gang favored.

"The Durans didn't see you cut up the trail," I said. "They'll be below us any second. They look mad. They're looking for a fight."

The clouds parted momentarily and we could see the line of Comanches, hard, dark men leaning forward as they drove their mounts toward the advancing Durans.

"So are they," Carmody said, snapping his revolver shut.

Like most battles, it was over in less time than you'd expect. With that many guns and combatants charging at close quarters, most of the killing took place in the first couple minutes. From our vantage point, we counted five Comanches down out of seven, and seven Durans down out of nine.

The survivors on both sides then realized it was time to take cover, and looked for a tree, rock, or dead horse to scuttle behind.

Before they could move too far, we finished them off. To a man, they died with a look of utter astonishment as the bullets rained down from above.

Chapter 24

For those not accustomed to battle, the taking of plunder seems barbaric. But when your life is at stake, and you come to the inescapable conclusion that the dead won't be needing the stuff anyway, you take what you can get for your survival in the moment and in the future.

We appropriated a good stock of pemmican – dried meat, usually buffalo, but it could be anything – from the Comanches, along with some dried berries that the Indians like to store up in fall. The Durans' camp was a trove of coffee, jerky, and most importantly, guns and ammunition. Good guns, too – some Sharps rifles and several of the new big-bore, single-action revolvers I favored. The Comanches' guns were older, probably cast-offs from the war with a few of them cobbled together from parts that didn't fit together very well. But mostly they were serviceable, so we packed them too. Their knives were excellent. It was late November and while the nights had not been particularly cold I sensed a change in the air and took a few of the warriors' buffalo cloaks, deerskin tunics, and boots.

Several horses were dead and we killed two who were wounded and suffering, risking making more noise with our gunshots. I felt bad killing the horses, and told Carmody so. He wondered aloud why I was concerned about a wounded animal but killed people without remorse.

I was going to argue that the horses hadn't intended to kill us and the men did. But in another life I would have told a student who said that to reconsider his shallow and superficial analysis.

It was a good question, and I didn't have an answer.

We picked the best four horses for use as spares and pack horses and headed back the way we came after taking some time to eat – for the first time in more than a day – and to groom, graze, and water the mounts. We now had a small arsenal, but there were only two of us and there was no time to hunt up reinforcements, even if we could find people willing to reinforce us.

What we'd do, exactly, when we got back to the Comanche camp was a good question, and I didn't have an answer to that one, either.

What I suspected was that about half the occupants of the camp had remained. It wouldn't make sense to leave the camp unprotected and at least one person would have to remain to keep an eye on Cassie, their captive, if she were still alive. Her fate was unknown at this point. Cassie served no purpose other than bait and her captives knew that we had no way of knowing whether she was alive or dead.

We had to go back to the camp, and we had to take a different route. Before long – if they hadn't done so already – the Comanches would begin to wonder what happened to their party and send out more scouts. By now, a blind mole could follow the trail we'd pounded out, and if we headed back the way we came we might run head-on into a war party.

Carmody suggested we follow a stream that cut off to our left. He's seen water near the Comanche camp, and while there was no guarantee this was the same stream, it was possible it was the same one, or it very well could be a stream that if we followed it would connect with the tributary he'd spotted.

We headed off. It was about an hour before sunrise.

Chapter 25

"Any ideas?"

"Lots of them," I replied in a low voice, worried about the sound carrying. We were maybe a quarter mile from the trail we'd followed before, and elevated a few hundred feet. From time to time we could catch a glimpse below, but only when the clouds parted. Even if the Comanches did come looking for the rest of their party there was no guarantee we'd notice them before they noticed us. But we had to plan, and we had to act soon, so we had to talk.

"Any that'll work?" Carmody asked.

"Probably not."

"Bounce them off me anyway. Let's think this through from the beginning. Just don't draw no more pictures in the sand with your little stick."

"Well, here's the basic problem: We know Cassie is being used as bait. We know they expect us to come get her, and the whole purpose is to kill us when we try."

"And we ain't even sure she's still alive."

"Correct. If they assume we've given up the chase they'll just come looking for us. She'd just be extra baggage."

Carmody thought for a second. "I think they'll keep her alive. White woman could be a valuable chip in all sorts of deals…if not this one, the next."

"I agree. Let's assume that to be true. Now, where will she be? They're not going to wait forever to find out what happened to the group that took off after the phony Duran. They're going to find those bodies, and I bet it'll be sometime this morning. But what then? Will they fold up and head back home, wherever that might be, and bring Cassie with them?" Will they go looking for revenge, and if so, who will they attack?"

"I don't think they're going to look for anybody besides us," Carmody said. "At least not right away. They could track the Durans' prints back to town, if that's where they actually came from, but based on what you saw there ain't that many of them left in the camp. You guess maybe half the Comanches set out after you?"

"Yes, but that's a guess. We killed seven braves and there were seven teepees, but not everyone would be inside a tent. Some would be on watch, others sleeping by the fire. If I were in charge, I'd keep half my men in place because I'd be afraid of an immediate follow-up if the attack was a diversion. Especially when they expect a raid to retrieve their bargaining chip."

"A Comanche would keep more men in place, I think," Carmody said. "They're crafty, and they'd be suspicious from the get-go. But they also wouldn't let an attack go unanswered. So I see your seven and raise you three. I think we'll be up against ten men."

"Not great odds. And they're sure as hell on alert now. And we can't just go in shooting – we have to get that crazy girl, get her on a horse, and somehow get back to town ahead of them. We don't know where to find her. Don't even know if she can ride a horse, or how well. And if she's there, I doubt that she'll be in plain sight. She might be in a teepee."

"Probably," Carmody agreed. "And we have no way of knowing which one."

We were high on a ridge and the dawn came upon us with unexpected swiftness.

Carmody was the first to spot the encampment below. I drew out the telescope, gave a look, and handed it to Carmody.

"We can't get much closer without risking them spotting us," he said. "There's an overlook down this hill we can reach by horseback. We could probably reach it without them sniffing us out but it's too far to get a shot. There's brush and woods all round the camp but we can't sneak up on them. It's their game and their table and we can't beat them. The same path you took last night leads right to the camp and continues past it, but that's wide open and they'd cut us down in a second."

"We need a diversion," I said, and came to a decision.

"You need to unpack all the ammunition we took off the Durans and match it up to the rifles and handguns. Load everything. And I need the four junkiest Indian rifles. No ammunition. In fact, pull the pins or jam the triggers so they can't be fired and used against us."

Carmody's gave me a hard look. "I got a bad feeling about this. You know what I'm afraid of?

I waited.

"That you're going to start drawing more of them pictures."

Chapter 26

I found a route down to the main path into the camp. I brought along the fastest-looking of the pack horses and hitched it to a willow about a half-mile away. I advanced a few hundred more feet, holding a stack of rifles under my arm, dismounted, and placed the butts in piles of dirt and carefully arranged the barrels and some tree branches I'd cut down. Then I checked my sidearm, the rifle I carried in my free hand, and the one in the scabbard. And then I took a deep breath.

Probably the last thing the Comanches would have expected was a crazy man galloping full speed into their lair. They heard me in plenty of time to pick up their rifles, but curiosity seemed to get the best of them and they waited to see what I was up to.

But then they heard the angry buzz of the bullets and the crack of the rifle fire above.

Most Indians are superb warriors but they don't fight the same kind of strategic battles as American and European soldiers. They're not particularly well-organized, and they think in terms of skirmishes and not tactical campaigns.

I was betting they wouldn't notice the lag time between the bullets and the shots, something I'd had drilled into me during the war. Major Thaddeus Munro, who commanded me and Billy Gannon with the Raiders, had drawn up a table of times and distance as they related to gunfire and made us practice and calculate. It was an odd thing to think of as I waited for a hail of gunfire, but maybe that's the goal of training – to insinuate itself into your mind and resurface when you need it.

Monro, who last I heard was a state senator in Texas, trained us to pay attention to the time between the buzz of the bullet and the snap of the gun. You generally hear the bullet first, because sound is surprisingly slow compared to the speed of big-bore rifle fire. If you hear the bullet and the crack doesn't come right on top of it, you know the round is being fired from far away, meaning it's more likely that the shooter will miss.

I guess the Comanches hadn't worked out that theory because they started diving for cover. They didn't realize there was little direct threat. Now, I won't say there was *no* chance that Carmody's shots would hit them but it would have been pure happenstance as he was probably a quarter mile away. No one – even Carmody – could shoot that accurately.

But he sure as hell could fire quickly. The shots cracked off like they were coming from a Gatling gun and the bullets fell like rain in about a hundred-foot radius, thudding into the ground and angrily snapping through leaves and branches.

It occurred to me that I'd better get down to business because the hail of bullets was just as likely to kill me as them.

I shot from the hip and killed the first Comanche who'd turned toward me. Firing a rifle that way isn't particularly difficult but it delays your second shot because you have to compensate for the recoil, which is generally much more powerful than from a pistol. I shot at another brave who was raising his weapon. I missed. So did he, distracted by the thud of a bullet digging into a nearby tree. My second shot caught him in the forehead.

There was no time to take inventory but I guessed there were about seven men left, and I was running out of options. I could keep exchanging fire, but the Comanches were retreating to a stand of trees a couple hundred feet away and once they got there and had some cover it was open season and I was a clear target. I couldn't very well run from teepee to teepee and peek in the flaps, so I bet it all on one roll of the dice.

One teepee, the largest, still had its flap closed. If Cassie were in this camp, I was betting that's where she'd be. I rode by, grabbed a handful of the hide, and tore the whole contraption out of the ground.

On occasion, time just seems to stop. I've seen that effect on the battlefield when a big shell lands, and despite all the mayhem everybody just freezes in slack-jawed shock and wonder. That's what happened. For a second, the braves froze as still as figures in a painting. I wanted to yell to her, but the words caught in my throat. Carmody's arsenal kept cracking and the bullets kept tearing up the landscape, but in those few moments a half-dozen men engaged in mortal combat were paralyzed, transfixed.

And horrified.

Chapter 27

I think he was their leader, maybe even a chief. Not all warriors wore bonnets, but chiefs did and there was a beauty on the ground near his head. It was large, made out of a buffalo scalp, and had a trail of feathers attached. The feathers looked red, but maybe it was the blood and not the bird that produced the color.

Cassie sat blinking in the sudden sunlight. The first thing I noticed about her were her arms, painted with blood to her armpits, and at first – uncomprehendingly – I had wondered why she was wearing shoulder-length scarlet gloves. Then I saw the knife. It was magnificent; Indians had good judgment in trade knives and preferred them to their own comparatively crude weapons, and the chief, or whoever he was, had secured a gleaming two-foot-long Bowie knife with a wicked hook on the end, a hook that would be sharpened on both sides.

She'd cut his clothes off before doing the deed with his own knife. I would guess she had snatched the knife, killed him quickly, and then worked methodically on dissecting him because he would certainly have made his displeasure known to others had the sequence been reversed.

Next to his war bonnet, nestled in the grass, were his eyeballs, white and round and seemingly alert in a nasty, life-like way. Apparently, they had been carefully wiped clean of gore. His legs were spread, and atop a pad made from a neatly folded buckskin tunic were his penis and testicles.

I held out my hand and Cassie took it and I hoisted her into the saddle in back of me. She hugged me tight; the knife was still in her hand and the point was uncomfortably close to my throat but there was no time to discuss it so I spurred the Steeldust and we headed back the way we came.

I risked a look back. You don't want to spend a lot of time looking back when you're running for your life because your attention should be focused on what's in front of you but my curiosity got the best of me. There were five of them left alive. They were getting their wits together and gathering their mounts and would be after us in a heartbeat.

She wasn't a big girl but an extra hundred pounds will slow down any horse, and we would need a sizeable lead in order to switch her to her own mount, which was staked farther down the trail.

"Can you ride?" I shouted.

"No one will ever do that to me again," she replied.

"Can you fucking ride?"

Her being crazy was going to make this difficult, although in all fairness the fact that she was out of her mind had enabled us to get this far, at least.

"I have a horse staked out for you ahead."

"Yes, I can ride." Her voice was strong and possessed of a lunatic calm. "But if we stop they'll be on us."

I unholstered my pistol and handed it to her.

"When I give you the word, turn around and fire. You probably can't hit them, but give them something to think about. All six rounds, as fast as you can."

She didn't question me or argue. Perhaps my plan seemed logical to her, in the unspoken code of insane people everywhere.

As soon as I spotted one of the rifle barrels protruding from the brush I ordered her to fire.

A full second later, bullets started humming and chewing through the tree limbs above us, and a full second after that I heard the reports of Carmody's rifles. I knew that he would essentially be firing wild, and there was a risk that his covering fire could hit me, but that would be a one-in-a-million chance. Hardly even worth considering.

And then, of course, one of his bullets sliced into my leg. It was a through-and-through flesh wound, I guessed, and my first thought was actually relief that it somehow missed the horse, but then I noticed the blood and knew I was in trouble.

Leg shots can make you bleed out in a hurry. It didn't hurt, though. The pain would come later, I knew. If there was a later.

Suddenly I heard confused voices, the irregular hoofbeats of horses being pulled up short, and rifle fire from behind me. The pursuers had seen the rifle barrels. I'd planted two on each side, protruding just enough to be noticed. They'd figure out it was a ruse in just a moment.

But a moment could save our lives.

I was on my own now. The plan was that Carmody would abandon his perch as soon as I passed the planted rifles and hightail it to the main trail. I'd be without covering fire for several minutes.

Everything depended on getting to the staked horse, keeping our lead, and waiting for Carmody to pull up the rear.

I felt my horse tiring and noticed that my field of vision was narrowing. It was like peering down two gray, narrowing tunnels.

A movement and a sensation surprised me. Cassie was pulling rounds out of my gunbelt and reloading the pistol.

"There's four of them," she shouted. "And they're gaining on us."

"Five," I said, and the words felt thick. "There's five of them."

"No, *four*. I got lucky the first time I fired."

I was going to say something encouraging but the words wouldn't come any more. I looked down and saw that blood had painted my thigh and the flank of the horse.

The Comanches started firing from horseback and all the shots, as far as I could determine, went high.

Cassie emptied the gun again.

"*Three*," she said.

I wanted to offer some words of encouragement but my mind and body wouldn't cooperate. I began to slide off the left side of the horse and I hit hard. I twisted as I fell and knocked the girl off, too. My rifle flew probably another ten feet from me. It might as well have been ten miles. The staked horse was a lifetime away.

The pistol I'd given Cassie was empty. I'd counted the shots. Counting shots is a soldier's habit.

Old habits die hard even when you're dying.

Improbably, Cassie still had the Bowie knife. She'd stuck it in the belt of her tattered and blood-stained dress and somehow it had not disemboweled her when she fell.

I was going to try to get the knife and kill her. It would be quick. There was no predicting the mood of a Comanche, but I believed that what they had in store for her after all this would be slow. Intentionally, methodically, barbarically slow.

I reached over and a bullet tore into my shoulder.

It was hot, I realized. We were in a wide, sandy clearing guarded by craggy rocks. It was late November but some Texas days could still be scorchers this time of year, and it looked like this one would develop that way, even if I didn't get to see it.

Heat and sun have always added to the agony of death, I think. Wounded men will sometimes use their last ounce of strength to crawl to the shade, if they can. I wouldn't have that opportunity, it appeared. If they decided to torture us for a while Carmody might save us, but the oldest Comanche, presumably exasperated by the whole process and wanting this to be over now, raised his rifle and aimed.

The hiss and slap was barely audible, at least to me, and the Comanche with the upraised rifle looked more confused than anything else. His eyes grew wide and he looked up without comprehension. As he turned in a stumbling circle, there was another hiss and slap and another Comanche dropped his rifle and reached both arms behind his back, clawing at something.

The older one fell flat on his face and the arrow protruded from his back at a perfect perpendicular angle. It stuck in the air like a flagpole. The second wounded brave fell backward; I heard the arrow snap as he fell on it.

One Comanche remained and he had his rifle to his shoulder. He spotted the archer atop the hill and raised his sights. The arrow went through his throat before he was able to get off a shot.

The last thing I remembered that day was seeing Taza climb down the hill and what looked to be a dozen Apaches sprouting from the rocks. He moved gingerly and I remembered that he'd still be nursing a fresh wound and a few broken ribs.

Taza came at me with a strap of leather and in the gloom of my seeping consciousness I wondered why.

Was he going to strangle me? Why didn't he just put an arrow through me?

He tied the strip around my leg above the bullet wound.

"We will fight," he said, "and I will kill you. But as you say, it will be another day."

Chapter 28

I woke up in Elmira's bed what they told me was four days later.

You'd think four days of sleep would make a man rested but I had trouble staying alert for more than a few minutes at a time. Every hour or so a face would pop into my consciousness, I'd do or say something, and then drift off again. I had trouble keeping the dreams and reality sorted out. There were some nice dreams about Elmira's face popping up in front of me. Carmody's face spurred some dreams about sea monsters and the like. There was a doctor in both my dreams and reality. He poked around doing things that vaguely hurt and fed something to me with a spoon. I didn't dream at all after I swallowed the stuff in the spoon.

It was probably a full week before I had all my wheels on the tracks. It seemed to happen all at once: I felt stronger, moved myself up toward the headboard, almost sitting up, and called for Elmira. I was hungry. And I wanted to see her.

Carmody appeared instead.

"What do you want now? For somebody who sleeps like a bear in winter you sure make a lot of demands."

"I was going to ask for something to eat but for some reason I just lost my appetite. Anyway, what happened?"

"I been telling you the same story for days but it just goes in one ear and out the other," Carmody said. "Are you ready to pay attention now?"

"I think so. I've been in and out. Go ahead."

Carmody swung a chair around and leaned his forearms over the top. "Firstly, you damn near bled out. From where I saw the first drops of blood on the trail I figured it was my bullet that hit you first. Sorry about that."

"One-in-a-million shot," I said.

"Yep. Go figure. And I damn near had a heart attack when I got to the pass and saw you was in the middle of a regular Indian convention. That Taza, the Apache…he was there and he held up his hand and I didn't do nothing. He probably saved your life with that tourniquet, an odd thing to do considering the beating you put on him. He didn't say it, but I think he was grateful you didn't kill him after that freak accident and he's waiting to finish the job of killing you the proper way someday."

I nodded and waited for Carmody to continue.

"Now, I got something unhappy to tell you. The girl."

I tensed, and when I did my shoulder hurt like hell.

"Taza 'claimed' her. That was his word. Said she was his now. And the damndest thing – she didn't kick. She said she liked the idea. That girl has squirrels running loose in her head."

"You don't know the half of it. Did she tell you what happened when I found her in the Comanche camp?"

"Only that you pulled her outta the chief's teepee. There's more?"

There was, of course, and I told him.

"*Shee-it,*" he said.

"Exactly. I almost feel sorry for Taza. How is Elmira? She must be frantic about Taza taking Cassie."

"She ain't happy, but she ain't real broke up, neither. She knows Taza, knows some of the Apaches, and used to live in the same camp with Taza's father. She thinks Cassie will be all right until you can get her back."

I wasn't in the mood to start planning that particular adventure yet, so I let him continue.

"You're new to these parts, and so am I, actually, but the story is that as much as the Apaches hate us, they hate the Comanches worse. This used to be big Apache territory right here, but the Comanches more or less drove the Apaches into hiding, and some of them way down into Mexico. That's why Taza was more than happy to make porcupines outta those Comanches when he got the drop on them."

It wasn't important, really, but I had to ask my next question.

"Why the bow, I wonder? Why didn't Taza just shoot them? The Apaches have plenty of guns."

"Funny you should ask, because he told *me* and told me to tell *you*. He still can't fire a rifle because the recoil hurts too much cause of where you busted his ribs and all. He says it sure takes a lot of pain to keep *him* from doing something, and hopes that you think about pain a lot – because he's going to lay some on you when you're both healed up."

"If you see him, let him know how I feel right now and he'll be happy that I'm suffering in the interim."

Something occurred to me as an afterthought.

"By the way, if I start poking around under the covers, am I going to find that most of me is still here?

"Your leg ain't all that bad," Carmody said. "Didn't hit the bone but cut some veins and you lost a lot of blood. The doc says your shoulder will heal up all right because the bullet didn't shatter the socket but you're going to be sore and stiff for a while. Months."

I began to get tired again.

"One more thing," Carmody said. He had trouble meeting my eyes.

I just let him say it.

"I have sort of a confession to make. Taza told me he spoke to you in English."

I didn't know where this was going and wanted to shut my eyes but Carmody was determined to keep talking.

"Well, Marshal, when you was having that fight with Taza I could *tell* he spoke English. I was stealing a glance or two and he was following our conversation. That's why I said all that brave Indian warrior stuff toward the end…trying to set up a graceful way for us to back out of there. I didn't want to tell you because you'd feel bad and sorta stupid but when Taza talked English to you that pretty much let the cat out of the bag, so I thought I'd let you know. I didn't see no harm in not telling you. I was trying to protect your feelings."

I groaned. He probably thought it was from the pain in my shoulder.

"Now I know you was a big-time war-hero type and all that, but one thing I've learned in fighting is to never assume *nothing*. Now, I didn't want to make you feel bad for not picking up on it, but since you know, I should remind you that Indians are smart."

He warmed up to his lecture and actually began wagging his finger at me. I debated telling him that I also assumed he was stupid as he assumed I was – but I didn't have the energy. I figured I'd save my strength until I could strangle him.

"In any sorta fight," he continued, "you never take what the other guy knows or don't know for granted…"

Merciful sleep overtook me.

Chapter 29

I won't say I had a stream of visitors over the next few days, but there was a pleasant, intermittent trickle. Elmira spent much of her mornings with me and brought up my food, and Carmody was in and out, busy, he told me, taking over my job while I was laid up.

People I didn't really know stopped by. The blacksmith, a broad black-haired young man with huge hands, name of Richard Oak, said he was a friend of Cassie's and knew her before her "troubles" started. He'd heard what I'd done to save her, and wanted to thank me. She was a troubled girl from the get-go, he told me, and had lived in constant fear of her father. He looked like he wanted to say more, and I wanted to know more, but my attention was evaporating as I began to feel weak again.

I got the impression he was still harboring a crush on Cassie, and debated advising him to go back to his shop and hammer himself out what the medieval armorers called a codpiece, but I held my tongue and drifted off.

The druggist I'd talked to briefly weeks ago pulled up a chair and inquired as to my health. His name was Vern Miller, and he was one of those sour and dour pickle-sucking-face types who I pegged as not being much fun but perhaps a steady presence when you needed him. Maybe he wanted an end to the town's trouble and was offering some tacit support. But he was still no help. I'd pressed him before on what he knew of town affairs and when he didn't want to answer he just didn't answer. I got the same cool stare when I revived the subjects of Eddie Moon, Mr. Adler, and Zach Purcell. I could live with that, at least for the time being. At least he wasn't lying to me, which was refreshing.

It was early evening after my first week in bed when I received a visitor I surely didn't expect. He didn't knock.

Toad filled the room. Even though it was now the first week of December and nighttime temperatures were dipping near freezing he still kept his sleeves rolled up to show off his muscles.

"If you came to finish what we started, you might win this one, since I can't stand up," I said. That wasn't exactly true as I kept my revolver under the blanket – Carmody had retrieved it from Cassie – and it was in my hand as I spoke.

"That's not why I came," Toad said.

"Why did you come?"

"To warn you. I don't like what's going on here, and I'm riding out."

"Why do you care about me?"

Toad crossed his arms, and with the meat in them pressed against his chest they swelled like ham hocks. "I don't care much about you, but just so you know, I'm not mad about what happened. You're a fighter and I'm a fighter, and that was business. You won fair and square even if you are trickier than you are tough."

He shifted his weight and thought for a second before he spoke. "You're up against a stacked deck, mister. I don't know exactly how and I sure as hell don't know why, but there are some pretty powerful people lining up against you and they want you dead in a hurry. They wanted you out of the way before, but you showed the bad judgment to hang on, and now they want you dead *yesterday*. Not only you, but Carmody and Mrs. Adler."

"The 'they' that want to kill us includes Eddie Moon, I take it."

Toad grew a little impatient. "Moon is part of it, sure, but he's just a chess piece like me and Dottie."

"Who's Dottie?" I regretted getting him off the track because he was a man with something on his mind, and it wasn't, from what I could see, a very expansive mind, so I wanted to maintain his focus.

"Dottie's my girl. She works at the Full Moon. I know she's a dove, and it don't bother me too much she's with other men, but some of them beat her up bad and that *does* bother me."

"Who beat her up?"

He looked like he was going to clam up and leave, so I hazarded a guess.

"Purcell." I made it a statement and not a question. It's easier to get somebody to agree yes or no than answer something open-ended.

Toad's face grew harder and angrier. His nostrils flared and it looked like he was smelling something bad.

"We always knew Purcell was pulling the strings," Toad said. "Just whispers, at first. We heard rumors that he was squeezing Moon. We figured that's why me and the others were hired, to put Mrs. Adler out of business so that Purcell would have more to wring out of Moon. Don't get me wrong, Moon is kind of a scummy guy in his own right, but I hear he got along with the Adlers for years."

"So why did he suddenly turn up the heat?"

"Don't know. I honestly don't. It don't make sense as it stands, and I'm sure you figured that out for yourself. There ain't enough money in all the businesses in town to justify bankrolling a bunch of hard cases trying to strongarm Mrs. Adler. Why would Purcell get his hands in this? And from what I hear, there are bigger criminals that Purcell pulling *his* strings."

"Like who?"

Toad shook his head. "That's all I know. I'm not trying to be cagey, Mister, I just don't know nothing more. I'm just muscle and low on the ladder. But I can smell something big at stake here. It don't take no detective to figure that out."

"One more question? You know what happened to Billy Gannon, the marshal before me?"

"I know he was shot. That happened a couple days after I was brought in. Word was that somebody wanted to keep him from going to Austin. Why he was shot, I don't know. What Austin had to do with it, I don't know either."

He moved toward the doorway. He was so wide he reflexively turned sideways to walk through it.

"I'm headed out. If you're smart, you'll leave, too. But something tells me you ain't that smart."

"Thanks for telling me what you know," I said. "Good luck to you."

He didn't reply and left the door open when he walked out.

Chapter 30

I'd never actually sent a telegram before. I've read hundreds, been handed them plenty, and told other people to send them, but when I began walking again I stopped at the telegraph office on the edge of town, the first time I'd been in a telegraph office, and wrote out the message and gave it to the operator. At first I didn't know how to contact the person I wanted, who to send the message to, and it took some back and forth messaging to narrow it down.

Each telegram cost about a dollar. I thought that was a quite reasonable price, especially as the telegraph operator said he'd just bill my office. I still wasn't sure who paid the bills at my office, so that sounded just fine to me. Over the next few days, I finally started getting hold of the right people and getting regular answers, and I felt guilty that the person supplying me with the information also had to pay a dollar each time to do it, but the fellow I eventually reached was a state senator and I guess his "office" paid for it, too. It was nice catching up, in any event.

The telegraph operator, a skinny old guy named McPherson, acted like he hadn't paid attention to my messages, although I'm sure he had probably made copies and passed along the contents. Deep-pocketed people like whoever was backing Purcell tended to want to know what was going on around them and I'm sure they didn't mind paying for the privilege.

And that was fine. Pretty soon I'd want them to know what I knew. Right now it was all guesswork on not adding up to anything, but soon I'd put the pieces together.

Meanwhile, it was fun sending out those messages and waiting to get ones back in. I could see how that sort of thing could get addicting.

Chapter 31

It had been exactly twenty days since I'd arrived in Shadow Valley, though it seemed much longer. I'd spent a good deal of that time laid up, and thus knew considerably less about the town than a marshal who'd been on duty almost three weeks should be expected to know.

As my strength returned, I floated the idea of a vigilance committee and got no takers except for the blacksmith, who looked like he could take care of himself. I had my doubts, though, because if as I suspected he had feelings for Cassie he would eventually find himself out of commission in more ways than one.

My problem was not only that the good people in town were too scared to help me, but I also had no firm idea who the good people actually were. Tentacles of evil entwine people who look good on the outside, and the good and bad teams were chosen long before I got here.

Choosing up teams always seemed to me like sort of an arbitrary process, anyway. Good people can be conscripted to do bad things. I'd spent four years fighting people who were defending the indefensible evil of buying and selling humans like cattle, but I can't say all the rebs, as individual people, were evil. As best as I could figure it, most were ordinary folk who against their will were plunged into extraordinary circumstances, and told by those in power to defend the only way of life they'd ever known.

In the past weeks we'd chosen up sides against a gang made up in part by Mexicans. The Mexicans in this part of the country often chose up sides based on the idea of keeping land they thought was theirs, and that's a motivation I can't hold against them. But like anything else, what you see depends on how you're looking and who you're looking at. When the Durans signed up to kill us, we thought of them as an historic enemy. But in many parts of the Southwest Mexicans made up some of the most fierce Union militias and saved the North's bacon on more than one occasion.

And also in the past couple weeks, events had conspired to make one Indian tribe my enemy and another my friend. They, too, were fighting because of factors beyond their immediate control, and beyond their making. I don't pretend to understand the nuances of the troubles between the Apaches and Comanches, nor the trouble between them and us, but it looked to me like one more case of assumptions gone crazy. Look at the trouble with treaties: We assume that the Comanches have some sort of central government and a treaty with one group was somehow communicated to all, but that's just not the way things work in their world.

Simple labels and categories save the mind from having to work too much and that's not a good thing. My theory was to judge people as individuals. And in just a few hours that theory would be put to the test when I would count on an ostensible enemy to be a friend.

I hoped I was working things out correctly.

But I had no doubt about the inherent evil of one enemy – an enemy who had once fought on my side. Rumors about Zach Purcell had been circulating for months, I gathered, but I had a hard time getting anyone, even Elmira, to go on the record about what they had heard. I suppose it was like asking townsfolk about witchcraft in Salem; the less said about the Devil, the better.

So I gave up playing detective, knowing that whoever was behind this had to come to me, now. I let it be known that I was waiting. And I'm sure the skinny old geezer at the telegraph office was undoubtedly spreading the word, too.

As to Purcell: I'd heard that he'd established himself as a feared and ruthless gunfighter, as well as a gangster with involvement in lots of shady stuff, including the dark corners of state politics. I'd known him a little during the war – as I told Carmody, he even repelled the other sadists and Billy Gannon went to far as to have Purcell relieved of his post – and heard some about him in the intervening years, but didn't have a handle on his reputation of late in these parts. While I'd been involved in lawing in several territories, and heard out-of-town news and seen wanted posters float across my desk, the Southwest is not like Illinois; there's not much centralized communication and in some parts of the territory the next town might as well be the next planet for all you hear from there.

All I knew was that I was Purcell's main impediment to getting what he wanted, I and Carmody, and there was a shit-storm brewing that was going to rain down directly on me.

In the meantime, there wasn't much I could do except try to get myself back in shape for when everything came down. I did want to help Elmira, and did want to get to the bottom of who killed Billy Gannon, and most certainly wanted the reward money. And I wanted to get to the spider in the middle of this bizarre web of fear and half-truths that dominated life in Shadow Valley.

But all that was secondary.

In the past 20 days, somebody had tried to kill me or get me killed so many times I'd actually *lost count*. There was a showdown coming, and I'd force it. I owed somebody that much.

And I was looking forward to the payoff. This was my type of game, and as much as I enjoyed playing, winning was the best thing of all.

Chapter 32

I spent the next few days target shooting. I found a nice open spot in front of a hill, just on the edge of town. The hill would absorb errant rounds to avoid anyone getting hurt by a ricochet or overshot. Several stumps provided me platforms for bottles and other things I could aim at, and there were several trees on which I could mount targets.

Word floated back to me that the townsfolk thought I was a bit eccentric, and some of the ones who lived or worked on that side of Shadow Valley took to watching me, leaning on fences, sometimes in groups, and as near as I could tell laughing at me a little from time to time.

I was more than happy to let them think I was crazy. There are occasions where that works to your advantage. And there was method to my madness, in any event: My shoulder wound had slowed my draw and affected my aim. I had no idea when it would heal completely or if it really would. So I had to get used to shooting the way I was, with what I had at the moment in the way of physical capabilities.

Wearing my holster about two inches lower helped. Not having to raise my right hand as high avoided the hitch I encountered when my elbow reached a ninety-degree angle and the backward movement of the elbow forced my injured shoulder to rise. I didn't like the looks of it: Men who wore extremely low-slung gunbelts always struck me as attention-seekers who wanted to look like shootists. But you do what you have to do, a phrase I had lately begun to use often because it irritated Carmody.

I'd left word around town that anyone who wanted to see me knew where to find me. That was an unnecessary admonition as I was pretty hard to miss, blasting away hour after hour. But I wanted the word on the street.

Nights I mostly stayed in my room at the lodging house. I avoided the Silver Spoon. Elmira had become sort of distant, anyway.

Carmody kept the peace and updated me from time to time on changes in town, most notably the influx of some new hard guys who were hanging around the Full Moon.

It was on the third day of my shooting spree that I learned Zach Purcell was back in town. Good thing, too, because I was getting low on ammunition, and so was the provisions store. I didn't yet know how much I'd spent because they accommodatingly billed it to my office.

It occurred to me that there would be more than one reckoning in my future.

Chapter 33

I saw Purcell riding up and tacked a target to a loblolly pine as he approached. I kept my gun holstered so as not to prompt any premature fireworks.

He looked and dressed the part of a shootist. There's no standard uniform, of course, but black seems to be the choice of fashionable murderers everywhere and he was dressed in it from head to toe. He wore tight black leather gloves.

Purcell was so ugly he was impressive; I'll give him that. His face was long and pockmarked, the hair that protruded from under his hat was so black it was almost blue, and he wore a thin mustache, trimmed thin. I'd never actually seen a shark but I hear they have eyes like his, small, mean, and penetrating. Maybe Purcell tried to copy their stare. Or maybe the sharks tried to copy his, seeing as how he was so good at it.

Purcell dismounted and faced me squarely. I don't know if he was ready to draw down but I wasn't – not yet, anyway – and lifted my hands a little, palms toward him.

"What's this all about, Hawke?" The voice was deep, seeming to rumble up from the bowels of the earth.

"There are people watching, Purcell. They're a ways away, but they can see my hands are nowhere near my gun. You seem to hold most of the cards around here, but gunning down a town marshal who has posed no threat to you is a hard charge to beat no matter how much you stack the deck."

"Didn't know you'd turned coward," Purcell said. "I always suspected some yellow in you, but you can't see that sort of streak 'til a coward turns his tail."

"I'll be ready for you, but just not now. You probably heard that I got a little ventilated, but so did all the assholes you hired to do it. I just need a little time to work the kinks out in my shooting arm."

Purcell growled. It was a real growl. Like an animal.

"You don't need to get no kinks out, you need to *get* out. Now. You and that overgrown mountain goat deputy."

Purcell took a step closer. "You got a grudge against me and I've made sure people know about it," he said. "I ain't done nothing wrong and I got a right to defend myself should you try to get the drop on me."

"What you're trying to set up might not be in your best interests, Purcell. I've lost a little speed but you're still no match for me. Want to try me on that target?"

I knew that when I walked to the tree I would be a pretty tempting target myself so I tried to put that out of Purcell's plans.

"Mind you, Purcell, we've got about fifty people with a lot of time on their hands leaning on their fences watching, so now's not the time to gun me down on the sly."

He said nothing.

"Three shots. Fifty bucks I can get a closer spread than you."

"Do it."

I stood square to the tree. The paper target was 150 feet away. I drew smoothly and shot three rounds from down low. One was within the bullseye, but slightly left of center. The other two were in the nine ring, one about two inches to the left and the other an inch and a half above dead center.

"You think you'll scare me off with your fancy shooting," Purcell said. It wasn't a question.

I didn't reply and walked over to pin up a new target. I took off my gunbelt before doing so, not wanting to give him any excuses or justification for claiming I was a threat to him. I tacked the new target a couple inches higher up the trunk. Purcell didn't notice the different positioning or didn't care.

I hadn't yet finished turning around when Purcell drew and fired. His motion created a hissing sound as the gun snaked out of the leather and the first shot went off while the barrel was seemingly still on the rise. Shots two and three followed like an echo, and his Navy Colt was re-holstered as quickly as it had been drawn.

There was no need to retrieve the target. I could see from where I stood that all three rounds were tight within the bullseye.

"Give me my fifty dollars and then get the fuck out of Shadow Valley," Purcell said. "Find some nice peaceful town to settle down in, collect the taxes, write a few summonses, and spend the rest of your years behind a desk or in your rocking chair."

I handed him the money and he put it in his front pocket, not bothering to count it and not breaking eye contact.

"You understand me?" Purcell asked.

"Let's say I got what I paid for," I said.

He drew his head back an inch, started to say something, but let it go.

"By tomorrow," he said, turning his horse back toward town.

"Count on something happening tomorrow," I said.

I waited until he was out of sight and the fence-leaners found some other source of fascination. I walked back to the tree and took down the target from the tree. Loblollies are common in East Texas but you don't find too many of them in Hill Country, and I was lucky to come across this specimen. It suited my purposes just fine, being one of the softest woods you can find, and on top of that, this was an old tree with a little rot on the side facing me.

My knife cut into it easily and I only had to dig around for a minute or two until I got what I wanted.

Chapter 34

The Silver Spoon was slow that night, so Elmira didn't have a good excuse to avoid me.

She was ill at ease as we sat facing each other across her desk and before I could start the conversation she began to cry. I didn't know why and didn't know what to do, and didn't even know what my role was in this latest drama. Technically, I suppose, I was her employee. In practical terms, I was her protector. And after that whiskey-soaked night before Cassie's abduction, I'd become…well, I'm not sure what I'd become, other than confused.

I picked up my chair and set it beside her and held her. She really let loose. She quaked and sobbed so hard she lost her breath and took in a few quick gasps before starting the process all over again. After a few minutes she composed herself, looked for a handkerchief which I could not supply as I'd never gotten in the habit of carrying one, and finally rubbed her nose on her sleeve in a gesture I would have more readily expected from Carmody.

"Sorry," she said.

"Don't worry about it," I said, for lack of anything better to say.

"I think you should leave." The suddenness of the remark seemed to startle both of us.

"Now? You mean you want me to leave you alone?"

"No, I mean I want you to leave here. Forever."

"Can I at least know why?"

It took her a minute to collect her thoughts, and then she spoke slowly and deliberately, like each word was a step on untrustworthy ice.

"Because Purcell's going to kill you."

"What makes you say that?"

"He was here today," Elmira said. "In this *room,*" as if the very thought of Purcell in the same room was bizarre and outrageous, like encountering a mountain lion in your parlor.

"Lots of people have tried to kill me recently," I said. "I'm still here."

"But you can't *shoot*. I heard what happened today, with the target and all. And he's not like the others. He's worse. A hundred times worse."

"What else did he say to you?"

"He says if I sell to Moon he'll let you live."

"Nice of him. And you told him what?"

She looked in my direction but didn't make eye contact.

"I told him I can't. I *can't*." She began to sob and her shoulders heaved. "I just *can't.*"

I was out of sympathy and heartily sick of half-truths.

"*Why?* He's offered you twice what the place is worth. All right, so maybe I understand your reasoning. I wouldn't want to be run off my business either, as a matter of principle, and might not sell even if it were ten times the fair market value. I get that. But I don't see that as part of the equation here. You say you won't sell because it's the only life you know. You say you can't start over. That's bullshit. There's something else going on, something a lot deeper, and God damn it, I've almost been killed a dozen times because of it and you *owe me an answer.*"

I realized I was yelling and took a deep breath.

"You tell me honestly and I'll help as best I can," I said. "If you force me to turn over all the rocks things might not go your way."

"I…" she stopped and took a deep breath.

"And I just have a couple more to turn over. What's under a rock is usually pretty ugly. I don't think either of us wants to look there. This is your last chance."

"…I just can't."

Chapter 35

I spent the next day getting ready for the last act of this peculiar drama, and maybe the final curtain of my life.

There was a lot to do, and Carmody was going to be a busy man. God bless him, when he wasn't focusing his energies on getting under my skin he was one hell of a lawman. He certainly must have been a terrific soldier, too. He didn't quibble, didn't judge, and didn't even blink when I told him what I thought was happening and where I thought things were headed.

All he did was retrieve a pencil and what looked like a piece of packing paper and write down a timeline in a surprisingly elegant script. He repeated it all back to me, accurately.

The bank had a clock visible through the window even when the doors were closed. We would set our time to that. Not being a railroad town, Shadow Valley didn't need much in the way of accuracy and the time was sort of an educated guess. Clocks were set to noon when the sun was directly overhead. But we needed to coordinate some arrivals and departures, so we borrowed a pocket watch from the general store for Carmody, who did not have a timepiece, and set it to bank time.

I retrieved a couple telegrams from the office late in the afternoon before it closed. I showed them to Carmody after he rode back in after making his contacts, and he nodded.

Whether it all added up to anything was an open question. I'd know shortly.

"Something tells me we might not pull this one off," I said. "And in times like this I have a standard speech I give to people I've dragged into hopeless situations, which is a surprisingly large number."

"Lemme guess," Carmody said. "It starts with the fact you are damn likely to get killed tomorrow and get me killed along with you, and you say no hard feelings if I want to back out, and it ends with me telling you to stop with the bullshit and I'll see you in the morning."

"Something like that. Thanks."

"It's my job. Your job, too, though sometimes I can't figure out if it's your vocation or avocation."

The silence was heavy. He looked at me in sort of a detached way. "Surprised that I know some big words, or are you taken aback by what I actually said?"

I didn't like where this was going but there were lives on the line, including ours, *especially* ours, and I wanted everything in the open.

"Tom," I began, suddenly aware that this was the first time I'd ever used his first name, "let's not kid each other – you're no stranger to killing."

"No, Josiah," he said, without indicating any irony at invoking my first name. "I ain't. And I ain't judging you, I mean that sincerely. I've killed a lot of people what needed killing. Did I get a thrill out of it? Yes, sometimes, I suppose I did."

"So?"

"So I came up hard, killed to eat, killed to live, and in the war, killed because they told me to. Tomorrow I'll kill or be killed because I have obligations, and my life is the sum of everything before it. It's the only life I know."

"*So?*"

"So, you had *options*. After the war you could have gone back doing whatever professors do, which I gather involves a lot of running at the mouth, or dealt cards, or run for office, or hell, you could have played the damn piano in any saloon in the country. But I think you got hooked on fighting and killing during the war. It comes easy to you now, just like when you killed that Mexican sentry."

I started to speak but he cut me off.

"I ain't saying you done wrong. Maybe you had no choice, maybe bopping him over the head would have made too much noise, but after you did it it didn't even *occur* to you that you'd just killed somebody casual as a man flicks a mosquito off their arm. You seemed surprised that I'd even brought it up."

"You're saying I like it too much."

"I'm saying that there's men like me that fight and kill and the thrill comes natural after the fact. And then there's men like you that *need* the thrill and then find reasons to fight and kill to get it. Plenty. But you, Josiah, are a different piece of work."

"Meaning?" I said.

"Because you think about it. You try to balance it all out, fit everything into a theory somehow. And you make it sound right. Maybe you *are* right. Or maybe you just talk yourself into it. But in the end I believe that *you* believe you're killing for the right reason. And you think that without people like you people who don't think about it – people like Purcell – would have their way."

"I do."

"Well, Sir," Carmody said, drawing himself to his full height and standing at attention, "I can't think it through or talk it through as pretty as you do, but that's more or less what I think, too. Some things is worth fighting for. A very few is worth dying for."

"And that's how it might play itself out," I said.

He nodded. There was nothing more to say.

Chapter 36

Elmira was incredulous when I told her we were going to meet with Moon and Purcell in the morning to discuss selling the Silver Spoon. I told her things were not what they seemed and I needed her cooperation, but offered no further explanation. I didn't really have one yet.

I also made it clear that she had no other option. We were due in five minutes, I told her. And then I took her arm and began leading her. Not roughly. But in a way that, I suppose you could say, left her no other options.

"You're scaring me," she said.

"Yes," I said. And that ended the conversation.

Chapter 37

Eddie Moon, Elmira, and I sat at the round table in his office.

Purcell sat in a chair near the corner. His eyes showed no recognition, no emotion, just a cold, hateful radiance, like faraway light from a distant, dark star.

Moon knew that something was going to happen and was smart enough to let me do the talking.

"Before we're through today," I said, "the future ownership of the Silver Spoon will be decided."

Moon raised an eyebrow. Elmira's lips parted and glanced from me to Moon and back again. Purcell didn't react.

"And there's one other thing," I said. "One man in this room will be dead."

I had their full attention now. Purcell blinked. Moon began to speak but I held up my hand.

"I'm going to start by telling you what I know. Some of it's fact, some is guesswork, but it all fits together and between us we'll fill in the rest of the pieces. You each know a piece of what's happened, but no one here knows the whole story. We'll figure that out now."

Moon shook his head. "What *is* this shit? You said you were going to negotiate the sale of the Spoon."

"And I will, Moon. But first you have to hear my story. And here it is."

I stood up. I did it partly for effect and partly so I could react if Moon or Purcell made a move.

"Moon, you're a pretty rough customer. This is a tough trade, and preachers and schoolmarms don't survive in it. Still, you managed to co-exist with the Spoon for quite a while, and your gambling was on the up-and-up – at least you didn't cheat more than most. Some people around town say they actually respected you. But all of a sudden you turned up the heat on Mrs. Adler a few months after Mr. Adler did his vanishing act. I wasted a lot of time trying to connect you with Adler's disappearance, and now I'm convinced that what happened to Mr. Adler was about something else entirely, which I'll get to in a minute."

"I had nothing to do with Adler's disappearance," Moon said.

"I believe you. I think that when Alder was out of the picture it became, coincidentally, the time to turn up the heat on Mrs. Adler to sell the property. And that's when Purcell took over."

Moon almost looked at Purcell for direction, but caught himself.

"I think you're a tough and resourceful guy, Moon, but you were up against organized gangsters moving in on your business. You're not the first man to be muscled out of his business, and you won't be the last. But that's not the issue. I could see what was happening right away, but the question I couldn't answer was *why*. Why did these thugs move in on you and then, under your name, try to get hold of the Silver Spoon?"

No one answered, so I took the liberty.

"Elmira," I said, walking over to her and tracing an oval on the table with my finger, "you own property that extends a few miles in back of the Spoon. You know that, of course, and you probably know every inch of it because you've been scouring it for a month. I hear you take a lot of rides back there to 'clear your head' and 'help you think.'"

She stiffened.

"But I'm not going to deal with that now. The most important thing, Elmira, is *this*."

I swept my finger straight through the imaginary oval.

"A *railroad*. There's a major line to be built right through your property. It's not public knowledge yet. These things rarely are. Deals are cooked up in private, connected people then position themselves in the right way, and the businessmen and the politicians get rich."

Elmira pointed to the table as if the drawing really existed.

"But how do you know this?"

"Low friends in high places," I said. "I *knew* there had to be some secret value to the Silver Spoon. At first I thought it might be gold, or silver, or oil, but Carmody checked that out and you're sitting on a big pile of worthless dirt and rocks. Not even good dirt and rocks. But I wired a friend of mine who's a state senator. He did some sniffing around and found out about the preliminary layout for the railroad line. I got the full story in his telegram."

"Why here?" she said. "Why a railroad here?"

"This may not be prime cattle country," I said. "This isn't even prime whorehouse country, or *anything* country, but there has to be a way for the cattle to get from the big herds to the big markets. The days of the cattle drive are numbered. It's all about trains and cattle-cars now."

Moon spoke up. He looked surprised and it suddenly occurred to me that he actually hadn't known about the railroad. But then again, why would Purcell and the people behind Purcell – if there were any, if it wasn't just a Purcell operation from the top to bottom – tell Moon?

"I get it now," Moon said, and his surprise seemed genuine. "And it's not so much the fact that the railroad would buy the land, it's the fact that the land along a major rail line is prime real estate for businesses, especially if there's a stop – which I'll bet was a part of this deal."

Moon looked at Purcell and Purcell glared back, his eyes issuing a warning shot, but Moon was too angry to reel himself back in.

"It would be more than cattle cars," Moon continued. "Passenger lines always run along the same tracks, they'll be a gold mine. Look at all the people moving to Texas. And to California. All the places *between* Texas and California. I knew something was up, but never figured that angle."

I rapped my knuckles on the table.

"There are a lot of angles at play here," I said. "And I'm just getting started."

Elmira looked worried. Moon looked curious. Purcell looked right through me.

"I came here to find who killed Billy Gannon. I know the answer now. It wasn't that hard to figure out once I nailed down the train angle, but what had me stumped was what this had to do with you, Elmira."

She was frozen like a statue except for her chin; I could see it quivering.

"You wouldn't sell the Silver Spoon and the ranch land behind it because your husband's body is back there, somewhere. Billy Gannon hid it for you but he was killed before he told you the details, if he ever intended to tell you. Neither you nor he would have known, at the time, that it was going to be an issue."

I was ninety percent sure that's what happened, but it was still a guess. When her eyes welled up I figured I'd guessed right. Now I'd posit one final theory as to the death of Bannister Adler, throw it down like an indisputable fact, and see what happened.

I almost hoped I was wrong. But I didn't think I was.

"Elmira, I think your daughter Cassie killed your husband, her stepfather. She did it because he'd been raping her for years and she finally snapped."

I'd honestly never seen anyone go that pale that quickly. Her hand went to her mouth and she made an animal noise, a wail of pure suffering.

Moon's jaw dropped, and Purcell's eyes widened.

"Bannister Adler had a reputation for liking young girls," I said. "I heard that time and time again. I'm just putting two and two together here, but *how else* do you explain a teenage girl driven to a homicidal rage at the sight of me? A new man in her mother's life, and maybe a new threat to her? Why would she castrate that Comanche, and tell me she did it because 'no man would do that to her again?'"

"You couldn't prove that," she said.

"I know. And neither could you. I don't know if you knew, or suspected, or tried to provide it, or confronted him, but that's not what interests me now."

"I couldn't prove that," she repeated.

"I understand."

I didn't understand, not really, not completely, but I needed to finish this. "And when you found the body, you turned to Billy Gannon for help. Billy was a hard-ass about some things but not always a stickler for rules. He would have figured justice was already done, good old-fashioned frontier rough justice at that, and I know that he would have had a soft spot for you and Cassie. He was like that. He liked to look after people who couldn't protect themselves."

She nodded several times, strange, tiny, almost imperceptible nods, as though she were afraid that larger movements would somehow jar something loose.

"And he buried the body on your land."

"Yes," she said. It was a whisper. Hoarse. She was ashen. Stricken.

"And when Purcell, through Moon, tried to force you into selling you couldn't sell," I said, "because you knew that sooner or later – maybe sooner – somebody would find that body and then the story would come out. Even if the flesh had rotted away, even the dumbest lawman would figure out where that one-legged skeleton came from."

Elmira looked straight ahead.

"You *tried* to find it. All those rides during the day. Out of character for you, I'm told. You never took much of an interest in nature up until the last few weeks. But you found out just how big a few square miles are, didn't you? A lot of it overgrown, and you have no experience laying down a search pattern and didn't really know how to look or exactly what to look for."

"No, I couldn't find it." Confession is good for the soul, I've heard. Her voice was calm and a little stronger, so I guess it was helping her.

"Sometimes I'd double back and find myself doing the same area twice or three times. It all looks the same to me."

"Well, it took Carmody an hour," I said. "Reading terrain for him is like reading a newspaper is for you and me. The body wasn't buried very deep. I don't think Billy had actually put the body in its final resting place. He probably figured he'd come back and finish the job later. But for him, there was no later."

No one said anything.

"And so…that leads me to you, Purcell."

The hard planes of his face rearranged themselves into a mirthless smile.

"And so…here I am, Hawke. What do you want to say to me?"

"You shot Gannon and I can prove it."

Purcell sauntered to the coffee pot and poured a cup. He took his time taking a sip and gently placed the cup on an end table after returning to his chair.

"I wouldn't push this too far if I were you," he said, his voice soft, but the words were gilded and gleaming with menace.

"Gannon would be a hard man to kill," I said. "I have a feeling you intended to lure him into drawing on you so he wouldn't make that trip to Austin. You figured he was catching onto the railroad deal. Why else would he be headed to the capitol? We knew the same people and he would have found out in a day. You knew that. You had every motive to kill him. Maybe you got second thoughts about doing your business with him face-to-face, or were just in a hurry, and so you ambushed him."

Purcell leaned forward. His smile grew wider and his eyes harder.

"Tell me the rest, Hawke."

"I don't know what would have happened in a straight shoot-out. Maybe you would have won; maybe not. But at the same time ambushing Gannon would not have been easy – maybe harder for you than killing him head-on. We used to say he had eyes in the back of his head. That was before you knew him, Purcell."

I paused a beat.

"Of course, that was back when he had two eyes in the front of his head. When you knew him, he only had one left, and it was pretty obvious. It was hard to miss, what with the bandages and fresh scars."

Purcell didn't like that and the smile disappeared.

"I guess his face healed up, and there was still an eye left in the socket, but that lamp was out for good after he caught that shrapnel. The Army found a spot for a one-eyed retread – running stockades. That's where you two crossed paths. Gannon's scars healed, and he looked normal, but the eye was shot for good, and he kept quiet about it. Not the sort of thing a lawman likes to advertise – a big blind spot on his right."

Purcell was standing now.

"Gannon died from four shots in the right temple. Who shoots somebody in the side of the head like that? Only someone who knew to lie in wait on that side. You knew it was more risky to confront him from the front or try to sneak up on the rear, so you hung in his blind spot until he walked by. I'm guessing the end of the alley across the street. Way back where no one, including Gannon, *especially* Gannon, could see you. The distance would be no challenge to a shot like you, and you could just slip away."

"You said you could *prove* it," Purcell said. "But this is all made-up bullshit about what might have been."

"Yes, it's conjecture," I admitted.

"But *this* is proof."

I pulled three pieces of metal out of one pocket and four out the other and slapped them on the table.

"People like you are creatures of habit, Purcell. Creatures of the past. You find something that works and you don't see any need to move on. That old Navy Colt you carry still uses balls instead of bullets. A lot of old-timers still prefer that load. Unless I miss my guess, you pour them yourself and make your own cartridges. I'll bet it's a superb load, never a misfire, and I'll also wager you change rounds every couple days to keep them fresh."

I pointed to the pieces of metal to the left. "These balls I dug out of the tree after you outshot me the other day."

I moved my finger to the right. "And these are the ones Carmody dug out of Gannon's skull. Same color, same weight, same scoring. I've had them tested, and they came from the same gun."

Purcell swept the bullets from the table. "More bullshit! Nobody can tell which bullet came from which gun."

"That's the problem with being a creature of the past, Purcell. You don't keep up. I had these sent to the U.S. Marshal's office. In the past few years the art of detection has come a long way. They use microscopes and acids to test metal and such, and they can match up bullets to the point where they're getting convictions based on the tests. Two so far in Texas. You'll be the third."

The secret to effective lying is to be specific but not so detailed so that you over-sell. I had thought about dummying up some lab reports and waving them in Purcell's face, but he was no idiot and he'd see through that.

He was right, of course. Yes, anybody can make a guess at similar loads and calibers and the metal looked like it was poured from the same batch, but all I had were mashed-up shards that for all anyone knew could have been broken-off horse-shoe nails. No one can match bullets to a gun. But if there was a chance he believed some of what I said, I at least could keep his attention.

I deliberately turned away from Purcell and leaned over in front of Moon. I drew some papers out of my coat pocket and spread them on the table.

"Moon, I'm going to offer you a deal, and frankly, I don't think you have much choice in the matter, but the ultimate decision is yours. It's a simple contract, and as you're a gambling man, I think you'll go for it. It says that if I die today, Mrs. Adler will sell you her place for twenty thousand dollars. That's a high price – more than you've offered – but a fraction of what you'll make in the long run. So If I'm dead, you get the Silver Spoon"

I turned my attention to Elmira.

"Mrs. Adler – Elmira – you'll sign it, too. If I die you get twenty thousand dollars. You could live very well on that. You could get richer keeping it, but with me dead you'll have Moon and Purcell in your hair and odds are *you'll* wind up dead, so if I were you, I'd sign."

She hesitated, and I answered the hanging question.

"No, you have nothing to fear from the discovery of your late husband's body. I can't guarantee the story won't come out, and maybe that's a good reason for you to move on to a new life, but no one is going to prosecute Cassie. As far as I'm concerned, it was self-defense, and as of this moment I'm still the marshal and the one who makes that decision. As for you, you had no direct involvement in the killing. In fact, the only person who committed an actual crime was Billy Gannon when he hid the body. But there's no law that can touch him where he is."

I noticed, to my astonishment, that in the midst of all this, Moon was actually poring over the contract. I like folks who are focused and attentive to their work.

Moon finished reading and spoke up.

"If you live, it says here, I 'forsake any permanently renounce any possibility of buying the Silver Spoon, and acknowledge that such a sale could not be arranged through an intermediary sale to a third party.'"

"That's right. That means that no one, not Purcell, and if there's anyone pulling his strings, not them either, has anything to gain by pressuring you. All the crooked deal-makers in Texas won't be able to lean on you because there's no way you can get control of the Spoon and the property through a puppet sale. It's all in the contract, and a judge in Austin will know all this."

Moon shoved the contract away with the tips of his fingers. "I don't expect all parties in this matter to give up that easily."

"You're missing the main point, Moon. The contract is based on whether I live or die in the next few hours. If I die, you get the Silver Spoon, you and your lifetime business partner, the 'other party,' Zach Purcell. That's a deal from hell, but you'll be no worse off than you are now.

"I don't get it," Moon said.

"I don't either," Elmira said. "Why would you be dead, and why would you staying alive solve the problem?"

I heard footsteps outside, precisely at the time I expected them, and reminded myself that if I lived through this, I owed Carmody a beer.

"Because if I live, Zach Purcell will be dead."

Chapter 38

oon looked at Purcell.

I took Moon's face in my hand and swiveled his head toward me.

"Don't look for him to tell you what to do. Sign it. You win – and win big – *either way*. If I die, you get the Silver Spoon. If I live, you've got a guarantee of no more gangsters leaning on you. The only way you lose is if you don't sign and I make it my business to tie you into conspiracy charges. I'll admit, that's a long and complicated road that I don't particularly want to travel. I like my justice quick. So you don't have much of a choice."

I released my grip and he signed.

I slid the paper in front of Elmira.

"I'll sign anything," she said. "I don't care about this place anymore, this bar and this bordello and this land is nothing but a *curse* – but for God's sake I don't want to see you get killed."

What she said startled me. I'd been prepared to threaten her, too. After all, if she didn't sign there was plenty of pressure I could put on her, including the fact that covering up her husband's death and conspiring to hide the body certainly *was* a crime, despite what I'd just said. It all depended on who was looking and filing the charges.

But she came at me in a direction I hadn't expected. We'd shared a few whiskeys and a bed, but this was the first time I'd heard anything from her that sounded like genuine affection. For that matter, it was a long time since I'd heard such a statement from anyone.

I spoke softly, and for the first time that day, spoke the unvarnished truth.

"It's going to happen anyway, Elmira. It *has* to be this way. And you can help me by signing."

I handed her the pen and she signed. Her hand trembled and the ink smeared as she wrote in a jerky script.

Purcell was caught unawares and didn't know what to do, so he did nothing and said nothing, which worried me because that's usually the smartest approach and I was hoping to rattle him but he remained stony and composed. He stood motionless, hands at the ready but not provocatively close to his gun, as I crossed to the door.

"I'm going to open the door and hand this contract to someone outside. He's a lawman, but he's not here to do anything but pick up this contract and file it with the state."

A deputy state constable named Tom Harbold peered over my shoulder into the room when I opened the door. I wanted him to be seen but not walk in. I didn't want trouble; not now, anyway.

"It's been a long time, Lieutenant," Harbold said. I'd known him from my unit and heard he'd been lawing in the area. Carmody had tracked him down. Constables made most of their wages collecting taxes and serving papers, and while picking up a contract and riding like hell out of town before anybody could grab it from him was a departure from his normal routine, a hundred dollars in advance buys you a lot of consideration and flexibility on the part of law enforcement.

"Yes it has. I wish we had time to catch up. Some other time."

"I hope so," he said, and he was gone.

I turned back to Moon, Purcell, and Elmira. Everyone was standing, now.

"I want everyone to keep a cool head. I have some people to introduce. They're armed, but only because they don't want to face Purcell defenseless. But the guns won't be pointed or drawn. There's nothing to be gained by escalating this, other than making sure everybody in the room winds up dead."

Purcell nodded but his hand was hovering over his holster and his fingers were limber and steady. Moon saw Purcell nod and did the same. His right hand was resting near the flap of his coat, the palm turned away from his body, and I figured he wore a gun in his waistband near the small of his back.

Carmody walked in, followed by Taza and eight Apaches. They were broad-shouldered men, not tall, except for Taza, but muscular and hard.

They were dressed in what I surmised was the Apache equivalent of businesswear: white tunics, buckskins, and vests.

Elmira gasped as the last of the group squeezed into the room, which by now was almost literally full.

It was Cassie. She wore a fringed buckskin dress and a bright blue necklace.

"This is Taza, and these are some of his people. The woman is Cassie. She is part of Taza's family now. I've hired Taza and his men to protect Mrs. Adler."

I looked at Purcell. "In case you don't know, Cassie is Mrs. Adler's daughter. So this makes the arrangement we're entering into both a business matter and a personal one. There's a contract that's been signed, and if I'm killed, these men will make sure it's honored. Purcell, I know you could round up a couple dozen gunmen and fight this out with the Apaches, but do you want all that trouble? All I'm asking is that if I die Mrs. Adler gets the money guaranteed in that contract and she's free to go about her life free of harassment."

"I'll see to that." This time it was Moon speaking. A roomful of Apaches taking your side does give one the courage to speak up, I supposed.

"Thanks, Moon. I believe you." And I did.

Some of the Apaches where talking among themselves and there was a buzz in the room. Taza took the opportunity to sidle up to me and speak softly out of the corner of his mouth. "No need for mountain man to translate for poor stupid Apache. I speak English. You make mistake underestimating enemy, thinking dumb Apache cannot speak English. You, big military hero. You are great fighter but maybe not such good thinker. Mountain man tell me that."

I let the blood pound in my ears for a few seconds and after I'd calmed down I turned to dismiss the Apaches but they were gone. I didn't even hear them leave, and it was a pretty good object lesson to those present that if you crossed Taza's men you won't hear them come *at* you, either.

Carmody was the last in the room and he shrugged and closed the door behind him.

"They're taking up positions now for the piece of business Purcell and I have to finish. They won't interfere. Neither will Carmody. They'll just make sure none of Purcell's men interfere. This is all up to you and me, Purcell."

Purcell finally spoke. "You seem to think I'm going to play along with all this. If I draw on a marshal, even a half-assed marshal I don't even think was officially appointed in a half-assed town that probably doesn't exist on a map, I'll be a fugitive."

"You have a point," I said.

I unpinned the badge and tossed it on the table.

"I quit. I'm a private citizen."

Purcell shook his head. "I'm not playing your games on your terms, Hawke. Go fuck yourself."

Telling me to perform that particular procedure seemed to be an obsession with people in this town. I told him as much, and then I shoved him back over the chair.

Chapter 39

He hit the floor hard and stayed on his back, his boots in the air. He knew that trying to scramble to his feet would put him in a vulnerable position during the awkward few seconds it would take him to rise. On his back he could kick or go for his gun, though his draw would be complicated by the fact that his elbow couldn't move back very far before hitting the floor.

"Think you could outdraw me from that position? I don't think so, but if you try, I *will* kill you, and it will be a justified shooting. Right, Moon?"

"That's right," Moon said. "Only way to end this fair is to take it to the street."

Purcell was a professional shootist and the only people who live long in that job know to keep things and themselves under control and act only when circumstances are tilted in their favor, but every man has a temper and a breaking point. I'd pushed him past his. He was red in the face and ready to explode and, as it happened, pretty much out of other options.

He picked himself up, smoothed out his clothes, wiped the dust from the back of his sleeves, and backed out of the room, his hand poised.

I followed him and we did an odd, slow minuet through the bar and out to the street: Both of us kept the other in sight, both of us were poised to shoot, even though neither expected to until we got outside. Purcell exited the batwing doors first and stood in the doorway for longer than he should have.

He was smart. He was stalling, letting his eyes adjust to the noonday sun, hoping I'd still be blinking when the shots were fired. So I shoved past him, our chests touching.

I walked into the street and then back-walked to the left. With the sun directly overhead there was no advantage to be gained by position on the street, and Purcell knew that, too, so we didn't fight over which end to stand on. He took a minute to scan the buildings and the rooftops, as did I. There were no men to be seen. They were there – everywhere, his and mine – but out of sight.

Purcell stopped when we were 65 feet apart. I was comfortable with that distance – and, yes, it was 65 feet and I knew that because after years of my particular work I can gauge distances pretty much to the inch, as I'm sure Purcell could, also.

There's a mythology that's sprung up in the dime novels about shootouts: The guy who draws first is the aggressor and the one who draws last is defending himself and gets a pass. In real life both parties tend to draw when they feel like they have the advantage because it doesn't really matter who draws first. In an actual gunfight, a lot of men who fancy themselves fast draw artists send their first shot into the air or even into their foot. What matters is who fires the first shot that lands.

And whether you are acquitted because you drew second in "self-defense" largely depends on how many of your friends were watching and how well you know the presiding judge.

But today there would be no justice system except the rough and final justice of the street, and we both knew it.

I suspect both of us also knew that I didn't have full use of my right arm. I'd actually held back a little when I target-shot with Purcell. I could have done better, but not by much. A shoulder wound takes months to heal, and some people never come back from it.

So I took some time to limber up my arm, flexing my fingers. I hunched my shoulders a couple times to make sure my jacket wasn't bunched up above the holster and wouldn't interfere with the draw. Purcell didn't wear a coat or a jacket, even though it was cold.

I flexed my hand again, stretching the fingers. Purcell couldn't help but notice, and he watched for what must have been a full minute. I'm sure he thought he was drawing on a man who, if not exactly crippled, did not have a right arm and hand that was at full strength.

And he was right.

And it didn't matter.

He began his move, smooth, taking his time, confident that he'd be able to aim precisely and get off a killshot.

He was still watching my right hand as he drew. Purcell was practically hypnotized by that stiff-fingered, waggling right hand.

The hand that I would not use.

I pulled my Cooper Pocket Double Action Five-Shot from my coat with my left hand. It's a beautiful gun, compact and with a wide and thick trigger guard that keeps it from snagging on cloth.

As I told Carmody the night he was mesmerized by my piano playing, you can do anything equally well with either hand if you practice.

And as I think I also mentioned to him once, twice, or maybe ten times after we'd had a few whiskeys, you don't need fancy holsters or trick rigs to get off a quick shot. Some of the best shootists kept their guns in pockets or stuffed in their waistbands or, like some cavalrymen, stowed in a sash, butt forward, for a reverse draw.

I didn't need anything so fancy. A small gun in a big pocket is as good as any rig and better than most.

I hit him in the chest before he got off a round. His shot went in the dirt, and I put two more into him, one in the chest and one in the forehead. He stiffened when the shot tore open his skull, and he toppled slowly like a felled tree.

Chapter 40

I didn't stand around to admire my work because I wasn't sure if someone was going to take a shot at me. I retreated under the overhang of the Full Moon, and waited.

For about five minutes all I could hear was the sound of my own breathing. Then I heard the batwings creak as Elmira bustled through and threw her arms around me. I wanted to stop her. The very last thing I needed if hell broke loose was to have my movement encumbered, but I didn't protest.

Nothing happened for another ten minutes until Carmody yelled that it was all clear. The shout came from on high somewhere, I couldn't tell exactly where. That goddamn giant squirrel was hopping rooftops again.

Then a door opened; then a window, then two, then three. The druggist pulled up the shade on his front window and in a few minutes I heard the ring of the blacksmith's hammer. In an hour the street was full of people and horses and real life – like nothing had ever happened.

And two things occurred to me.

First, I'd never seen the town hum like this in the entire month I'd been here. It was suddenly a *normal* place. People were going about their business as though this were a *normal* town where people could come and go as they pleased and not have to cower from thugs and goons. And all this was happening while Purcell lay dead in the street.

The second thing that I realized was that the town of Shadow Valley still didn't have an undertaker and everybody was waiting for me to pick up the body.

Chapter 41

I decided to stick around town for a while, and so did Carmody.

When I pinned my badge back on Elmira told me that she would flush the town council out of hiding and get things on the books for real – "officially official," as she put it.

Most nights I stayed with Elmira above the Silver Spoon, though I kept the room at the hotel. I guess it was a comfortable relationship as far as it went; neither of us was in a hurry to take it further and frankly there was a lot of unexplored and maybe treacherous terrain that we'd have to navigate in the future.

We took a few steps into that uncomfortable, uncharted territory on Christmas Eve. The Spoon was decorated with a Christmas tree, and in a sure sign of prosperity the tree was festooned with gingerbread men. People on the frontier generally *ate* their food, so when they hung it on a tree, things must have been looking up.

Christmas had become a much bigger event since the war. President Grant had even made it a federal holiday.

I was playing carols on the piano and Elmira was sitting beside me on the bench. She tried singing. I know a bit about music and I can tell you the word "tone-deaf" is over-used. Very few people are actually unable to differentiate pitches but damn it, she was one of them.

I knew the words to a few carols, and sang one that had recently become popular, "We Three Kings." Elmira commented on how unusual it was for a man like me to sing and play the piano. It didn't make me angry, exactly, but I did want to know what she meant by "a man like me."

Things turned frosty. She didn't answer – we both knew what she meant – but instead volleyed back a question of her own.

"Does it bother you," she asked, "that I lived with the Apaches and had a baby with one? That I was a whore? That I run a whorehouse?"

"No," I said. "You didn't have any alternatives. You sure as hell couldn't make a living as a singer."

Neither of us spoke until I'd finished another song.

"Look," I said, "I don't make judgments based on assumptions. I judge people, of course, but I try to do it on who they are, not on who I *think* they are. Sometimes you get assumptions set in your mind so deep that you don't even know you made the assumption in the first place. They become invisible. They obscure alternatives to themselves."

The way she looked at me I could tell she didn't get what I was saying.

"Take Purcell. He just *assumed* that I was going to shoot right-handed, and that assumption killed him. It blinded him to the possibility I'd fish a gun out of my left-hand pocket."

I thought about what I wanted to say next and then spoke deliberately and softly as I played. She had to lean close to hear me.

"You brought up the Apache thing, and I know Cassie's on your mind. I never had children, and I would never presume to tell a parent her business, but I suspect that pretty soon you're going to ask me about getting Cassie back and I'm going to advise against it. One of those assumptions we make is that our way of life, our way of thinking, is better because it's what we know. *All* we know. From our view, a comfortable life, what we call 'civilized,' is always better, and has to be better for everybody. But for some people with too much to think about it's probably better to focus on the day-to-day. I saw that in the war. I can't prove it but I think a lot of very troubled people are considerably more at peace with themselves when they are fighting for survival."

"I guess some people just need to fight to feel alive," Elmira said.

I knew that was directed at me.

"But I pick my fights. And I like to think I produce a greater good in the end. I think the good guys won this one. You've got your business back, for one thing."

She laughed and the tension broke.

"I'm not sure that's such a good thing. The Full Moon's packed. We're not. He's running me out of business anyway."

"I can't shoot all your rivals for you. As long as he runs a legit business he can stay. Although it wouldn't hurt if he'd bribe me now and then."

"I guess you have to choose your battles."

"That is for sure the truth," Carmody said in a booming voice, startling us from behind. I stopped playing. I didn't know how long he'd been listening but I was sure of one thing: he was drinking whiskey right out of the bottle, the bottle was near empty, and he was very much in the holiday spirit.

"You have to pick your fights," he said, waggling that goddamned finger at me again.

"You pick your causes," Carmody lectured expansively, "you do the best you can, and sometimes you have to live with the lesser of the two evils."

"It's far from a perfect world," I agreed.

I'd had a few drinks and was not averse to being a little expansive myself.

"But maybe someday things will be better. Smarter people than me will really figure out how to match bullets to guns and we can put all the killers in jail, which seems like a big step closer to a perfect world as far as I'm concerned. Maybe we won't have wars, or at least we figure out ways to keep three times as many people from dying of sickness as from getting shot. Maybe we won't fight over land, or fight because we're from different places, or different tribes. And maybe we'll be able to fix all sorts of sickness, including sickness of the soul."

I didn't mean to say that last part but I've always had the tendency to fall in love with the sound of my own voice – and deep down I truly, sincerely, did hope that something could be done for Cassie.

If Elmira caught my reference, or if it bothered her, she didn't show it. She suddenly clapped her hands for attention.

"Do you have that watch on you?"

Carmody dug the timepiece out of his pocket. It was the one we'd borrowed from the store and I bought it for him with some of the reward money I'd collected when I turned in Purcell's body and identified Purcell as Billy Gannon's killer.

For now, that's all I knew for sure about Purcell – that he ambushed Gannon. Whether cashing in on the railroad scheme was his solo plot or if someone was pulling his strings was a secret that died with him. I said nothing to Elmira but I was betting there were other players in this drama and that the curtain would go up on a new act sometime in the future.

The watch wasn't cheap. Neither was my telegraph bill. But I pay my debts.

Carmody fumbled with the cover and squinted while he tried to bring the hands into focus.

"It's precisely twelve-oh-two."

"Then it's Christmas," Elmira said. "Right here, right now, it *is* a perfect world. Or we can pretend that it is, anyway. Maybe we can pretend again tomorrow, and the day after. Maybe we can fool ourselves for a while. And keep trying."

"That's the best you can do," Carmody said. He took another drink.

"That's *all* you can do," I said. I turned back to the piano.

THE END

About the Author

Carl Dane is a career journalist and author who has written more than 20 nonfiction books, hundreds of articles, and a produced play. He's worked as a television anchor and talk show host, newspaper columnist, and journalism professor.

He was born in San Antonio, Texas, and has maintained a lifelong interest in the Old West and the Civil War. He is a member of The Sons of Union Veterans and has traced many of ancestors not only to the Civil War, but also to the War of 1812 and the American Revolution.

Carl often writes and lectures about ethical dilemmas, and has a deep interest in morality, including questions of whether the ends justify the means and how far a reasonable person can go in committing an ostensibly wrong act to achieve a "greater good."

He has testified on ethical issues before the U.S. Congress and has appeared on a wide variety of television programs, including Fox News' *The O'Reilly Factor*, *ABC News World News Now*, *CBS Capitol Voices*, and CNN's *Outlook*.

Carl is also interested in the structure of effective and eloquent communication, and has written two recent books on professional writing and speaking for a commercial academic and reference publisher.

Reviewers have consistently praised his work for its deft humor.

When not coyly writing about himself in the third person, Carl lives in suburban New Jersey, where he is active in local government and volunteer organizations. He is the father of two sons.

The characters of Josiah Hawke and Tom Carmody – and the situations they confront – were drawn from the author's interest in the darker sides of the human soul, and the contradictions built into the psyche of every man and woman.

Hawke is an intellectual, a former professor of philosophy, who became drawn to the thrill of violence after the life-changing events of the Civil War – which not only exposed Hawke to violence but showed him that he possessed considerable untapped skill in that area. Carmody, yin to Hawke's yang, is a blunt backwoodsman who is no stranger to violence, either, but has fought for survival and not for sport. Carmody wonders if Hawke's philosophical justifications are merely a smokescreen for seeking out trouble – and he's not afraid to tell that to Hawke.

Follow Carl at www.carldane.com

www.ingramcontent.com/pod-product-compliance
Lightning Source LLC
Chambersburg PA
CBHW030924060726
47591CB00005B/1651